The Wichi... all six stor... downtown. Coal Barge opened the door and I saw Bull Granger sitting behind a gray metal desk. He was a big man with a flat face and a neck the size of a stovepipe. I could tell he was mad, because the veins in that neck stuck out like ropes.

"Sit down, scumbag." I sat.

"You tell me what you're doing outside my daughter's house. Then you tell me it won't happen again ... or I'll see you sit in jail till your mother forgets you exist."

"You got a charge, Colonel?"

The Bull got up and walked in front of the desk and slapped me full across the face. I didn't move. He looked at Coal Barge. "Escort this fried peckerwood out to the street."

"Colonel," I said, "you touch me again and you better kill me."

As I turned to leave he said, "You got a deal, peckerwood."

# HOT SUMMER, COLD MURDER

**Gaylord Dold**

AVON
PUBLISHERS OF BARD, CAMELOT, DISCUS AND FLARE BOOKS

AVON BOOKS
A division of
The Hearst Corporation
1790 Broadway
New York, New York 10019

Copyright © 1987 by Gaylord Dold
Published by arrangement with the author
Library of Congress Catalog Card Number: 86-91001
ISBN: 0-380-75058-9

First Avon Printing: April 1987

AVON TRADEMARK REG. U.S. PAT. OFF. AND IN OTHER COUNTRIES, MARCA
REGISTRADA, HECHO EN U.S.A.

Printed in the U.S.A.

K–R 10 9 8 7 6 5 4 3 2 1

For my mother with love...
(And to Bob Mitchum, of course.)

# HOT SUMMER, COLD MURDER

# ONE

It was hot and dead and still. The ceiling fan circled in a futile gesture, casting shadows on the pair of feet I had solidly stacked on my desk. I watched a shiny blue fly do kip-ups and a few twirls from the phone to the phone book and back. Once in twenty minutes it did a pirouette through a smoke ring I drifted between my feet, then settled back on the phone book rubbing its back legs in satisfaction. In the same twenty minutes one beat-up Plymouth cruised past on Lincoln Street and no one went into the barbershop next door. When it was that hot and dead I always drank sweet muscatel and when it got bad enough I thought about my ex-wife, Linda. After five years the memories never got any better.

I don't remember meeting Linda, being introduced to her, or even asking her to a drive-in movie or for a Coke at the drugstore. One day there it was. I was like Gregory Peck in that Hitchcock movie, when he wakes up as the chief honcho in a nuthouse. He can't remember his own

1

name or where he came from or how the hell he got to be chief honcho of a nuthouse. There's just this disquieting feeling that he better string along with the show or turn himself in. So he reads a little psychotherapy. He tap-dances around Adler and looks at the pictures of ids and egos. He is ready to go, and the doctors and nurses can't tell the difference. The patients think he is terrific: he has this natural sympathy and doesn't gum up the works with all that technical jargon which makes them feel sick. Everybody thinks how therapeutic it is that he can be like one of *them.* Well, Ingrid Bergman knows he's not one of them, because she wants in his trousers; Leo G. Carroll knows he's not one of them, because Leo G. Carroll is evil and therefore possesses a clarity of vision. But when it came to the movie version of Linda and me, I played all the parts. That made it harder to wake up.

I know what Linda had for me. In that other summer five years ago she owned an air cooler. It was a green whale beached in a tiny west window, chugging cool damp air and, leaking rusty water. I lived for that air cooler. That summer I was the chief honcho and sole inmate, but there was no Ingrid Bergman wanting in my pants—and no Leo G. Carroll sporting a pencil mustache and toting a gun in his coat pocket. There was nothing to refer to, so I worked and drank muscatel and listened to the Browns on KMOX out of St. Louis. Linda was a ghost who made me fried baloney sandwiches with mustard. I felt bad about all that.

For eight hours a day and four on Saturday I was a thirty-year-old stock boy at the Fox-Vliet drug warehouse at Oliver and Lincoln. I moved streptomycin, Vicks, and Halo shampoo off the loading docks and down the incline ramps, unpacked the crates, and repacked cartons for ship-ment to drugstores at retail.

I left work every day at four-thirty, my face and arms covered with grimy bits of excelsior, and drove north to Linda through the wasted summer streets of Wichita. I knew what I had to do, how the dream would start, and how it would probably all turn out.

I stopped at the Shoe's for wine. Kenny Shoemaker. The Shoe ran a broken-down liquor store on Hillside. Next door was the Uptown Recreation, a pool hall and hangout for snooker sharks and the boys with peel-off suits. Most of the Shoe's business was guys buying pints to mix with the beer they bought at the Uptown. There was never any trouble with the Shoe. He cashed checks and held on to them for ten days. For a guy with a decent track record, there was credit when he came up a little short. In a pinch, the Shoe would pass a case of Pabst through the back door on Sunday morning, then follow you home and help you drink it. When he got drunk and collapsed into his rocker in the back room, he left a sign by the cash register that said, "Make your own change. Shoe." Shoe stacked all the wine in a sun-scorched window where the labels faded and the wine turned sour. No one cared. Shoe sold mostly whiskey and beer. I had been there the day the Shoe started his "charity fund-raising drive" by putting three quarters in a plastic iron lung on a card with a picture of a crippled kid. There were still three quarters in the iron lung, but the picture of the crippled kid had faded like the wine labels until it was just a crutch and a pair of glasses. The Shoe got up and held the door open for me as I went in.

"Hey, Shoe! How's it goin'?"

"Mitchie, my boy." His mouth was a yellow cave, one teak-colored stalactite incisor holding on for dear life. He was a scrawny gray bird in a string tie and a cowboy shirt, and when he spoke he stuck his beak in my face and looped a bony wing around my neck.

"Mitchie, where you been, how you feelin'?" I was always at Fox-Vliet and I always felt like dropping a Girl Scout on her head.

"Pretty good, pretty good. You?"

"Mitchie, I tellya. I was out at the Rock Castle the other night and some old red-haired bitch got ahold of me. We was out in the parking lot. She was sucking on me, and I thought the fuckin' world was coming to an end. Shit, I was so fucking drunk. Shit!"

"Helluva deal." I looked at the first dollar Shoe ever made taped to the cash register, then at a picture of the Shoe and his wife on their wedding day in 1931, a yellowed clipping from the *Wichita Eagle.* Hands joined, they were holding a knife over an elaborate wedding cake. The Shoe looked about eighteen years old and had a big, wide smile. I realized that the Shoe and I were stumbling through the same darkened charnel house and there was always somebody around to keep score of the bumps and bruises.

I said, "Gimme a fifth of muscatel and a six-pack of Pabst."

"Need some cash?" he asked.

"Thanks, Kenny, not today."

"Whatcha up to tonight, Mitchie?"

I realized I was going to tell the Shoe that I was not up to much tonight—except that I would probably drink some muscatel and listen to the Browns on KMOX.

The Shoe grabbed the glass door and held it open for me. On the way out I passed a pimpled kid with a wispy brown beard. He wore a painter's cap and smelled like he had covered the world.

"Hey, Shoe! How's it goin'?" I heard him say. I fired up the Ford and headed north on Hillside to Linda and the air cooler, choking down the urge to open the muscatel right there.

Linda's place was a brick duplex slapped up during the war for families who came to town to build airplanes at the plant. Square and low. In the summer the place was like a basement and smelled worse. More than anything, though, the joint was cool and Linda's Philco picked up KMOX from St. Louis.

I sat down at one end of the couch, unfolded the evening *Eagle,* and lit a Lucky. Linda nestled beside me. I handed her the crossword and poured myself some muscatel in a glass with a picture of Big John and Sparky on the side. Sparky was a goofy-looking cross between a little kid and a gopher, and I covered his face with muscatel up to his floppy ears. The muscatel always tasted a little like peanut butter.

I never knew whether Linda really loved crossword puzzles, but she worked at them with the dedication of a fisherman at a dry hole. Her face would grow perplexed and she would slowly, thoughtfully, push a red fingernail into her mouth. Her sneaky brown eyes were almond-shaped, her lips luxurious but always pulled tight. In the perpetual dim summertime of the apartment, I thought she looked like Gloria Grahame.

"Mitch, what's ochre? It's a clue."

"A color. Somewhere between umber and sienna."

"No, seriously. Come on."

"All right," I said. "Say it's a vegetable cultivated mainly in the South." This was about the best I could do.

"Fuckhead!"

Usually I would go on for hours free-associating at Linda's expense. Tonight, though, something was up and serious.

"Actually," I said, "it really is a color. How many letters?"

"Six."

"Oh. Well, ochre comes out of the earth and can look like it—the earth. Something like yellow or orange."

"Those both have six letters."

"Well, work around it." God, oh God, I wondered if the wheel was invented by some guy trying to make a raspberry Lifesaver. I took my first big gulp of muscatel.

It was getting to be seven o'clock. I switched on the Philco and watched the yellow light around the dial gradually grow brighter, heard the hum and the buzz, the sound of the radio focusing on St. Louis and, finally, the steamy, faraway voice of Phil Stevens saying how Budweiser was the beer all the Browns drank. They must have drunk a lot of it, because they all played baseball like they were smashed.

The Browns were playing the Indians: the dirty Ohio River and the mighty Muddy in turgid confluence. Linda got up then. If I was lucky, the game would be into the bottom of the fourth before the beer and baloney sandwiches were served.

But something was definitely up. Instead of heading to the kitchen, Linda went to the bathroom and took a long shower. The water ran for an inning and a half. Then there was a frightening, virginal silence. I was sweating and had lost track of the ball game somewhere in the fourth inning.

"Linda? You all right?" Nothing.

The bathroom door opened. In the wedge of light, Linda floated like a blue butterfly. She wore an ankle-length satin kimono sashed at the waist. Her long auburn hair was looped into a single braid down her back. She was trying to swish and glide. A hundred years went by, and I felt circles grow black beneath my eyes.

"Linda?" I wanted to make sure it was her.

"Mitch, sweetheart, dinner is ready."

That night Linda made meat loaf. I sat at the dinette while she swayed around the table, serving corn on the cob, white bread and butter, a jar of dill pickles. Finally, the meat loaf appeared. It looked like a muddy football decked out on a plate of forsythia. The thing weighed a ton. Linda forgot to put catsup and eggs in with the hamburger and it was like eating drywall. I wanted to ask her for some sand to put on top.

Linda talked about her mother's disappearance the week before. Someone found Mom's wallet in the parking lot at Maule Drugs and called Dad who called Linda's brother who called Linda. Suddenly Linda's mother was kidnapped, raped, and murdered. The police were called in to investigate. Actually, the police was some twenty-two-year-old kid who probably played fullback once at North

High. He looked me up and down and smelled muscatel and a rat. An hour later I was no longer a suspect. Linda's mother turned up at home complaining about her lost wallet. But there were still several hours in there somewhere that remained unexplained and everybody in the family had a theory. Linda thought her mother was in a religious crisis, though I could not figure out what kind of crisis a Southern Baptist could possibly have.

Linda stopped. Then: "Mitch, you don't have to go home tonight." I always went home after the Browns finished, played through a few chess games, and went to bed. By then the night was cooling down and, half drunk, I could sleep.

"Okay," I said. I saw myself chained for life to a meat loaf.

"Then come along to bed." She left.

The Browns and the Indians were tied in the ninth. I gulped the last of the muscatel. I followed a gulfstream of perfume into the bedroom, thinking about the bottom of the ninth and the good old days of fried baloney and Pabst.

In the faint light I saw Linda lying on her side covered by a sheet and two blankets. The bedroom air was a motionless, murky syrup. I undressed slowly, straining to hear Phil Stevens above the steady din of cicadas, the chug and clank of the air cooler. By the time I was naked, the Browns were threatening with two men on and none out.

"Linda, could we put on that little lamp in the corner?" If it was going to happen, I wanted to see it.

Linda said, "No, I'd rather we didn't."

"What?" I said.

"I'd rather we didn't put on the lamp."

"Why?" Perched on the scaffold, the condemned man discusses any topic whatsoever with his executioner.

"I don't want you to see my face." I felt the shame and fear in Linda's voice and felt sorry for both of us, for the loneliness she wrapped herself in, for the advantage I took of her weakness. I wanted to make things right by her.

I curled up behind her question-mark shape and lightly kissed her cheek, feeling with my lips how she held her jaw clamped shut, seeing in the streetlight and shadow the lines etched around her tightly closed eyes. She clutched the sheet and two blankets in a bunch beneath her chin. In the living room the Browns pushed a man to third, sending the Indians's manager, Billie Joe Walker, to the mound.

If Billie Joe could go to the mound, so could I. I touched her shoulder gently, rolled her over onto her back, and with my left hand pulled down the sheet and blankets before she could protest. She still wore her kimono, sash done up in a double half-hitch, her ankles locked. I knelt over Linda like a catcher behind the plate and jammed a sweaty right knee between her legs at the thigh. She relaxed, then tensed again. We were like those love bugs you see in the summer, wedded at the butt in a perpetually lewd embrace, the monster with two backs, an embellishment on the world's absurdity. Billie Joe Walker was at the mound again, the fans screaming for a walk. A Browns fan knew both limit and potential.

With the grim determination of Tamerlaine, I braced myself with two hands against an outcropping of pelvic bone around Linda's hips, raised my left knee, and brought it down between her ankles, working it in like a corkscrew and, at the same time, walked my right knee northward toward her crotch. I wondered if Linda heard the fans bellow at ball one. I used my right leg as a church key, prying at her thighs, gradually inching my left leg between her calves, then on until I felt my left knee between her own knees. I pressured her hips, pushing down and slightly out. The dangerous operation required speed and grace, power and finesse. Phil Stevens's beery voice rasped out ball two.

Suddenly, Linda's ankles popped loose and her legs flew open like a pair of scissors. She hissed like a cornered cat. With my knees delicately balanced on her thighs, my hands still grasping her hips, I bounced her twice against the bed with my whole weight and when we left the sheets for a brief second, I jerked the kimono all the way up around her belly. Before she could rally, I swallowed a quart of syrupy air and pushed myself backward and down, sliding on sweat, until my nose came to rest in her hillock and my shoulders were firmly entrenched between her thighs. I wrapped my arms underneath her legs and dug my hands into her bum. I curled an eyebrow up over the tree line and took a look around.

Linda still grimaced.

"You're not going to do *that?*" she said. There in Linda's bedroom, buried in the hooting and yelping of cicadas, buried in the misty depths of Linda herself, I did what Linda couldn't bring herself to say.

The Browns won the game on a wild pitch with the bases loaded. Later that summer the Giants caught the Bums and went around them on the miracle of Bobby Thomson's home run. It stayed hot in Wichita and, one dead Friday evening, Linda and I drove the Fairlane down to Nowata, Oklahoma, and were married in a little drive-in chapel. The Reverend Bob Smart officiated. The good reverend ran a mortuary in the basement and, as we left, he gave me his card. "We marry 'em and bury 'em."

Fall brought cooler weather and a divorce. The Shoe loaned me a grand for my investigator's license and a few months' rent on a little office along Lincoln Street. Mine was a small life, skip-chasing, repossessing Pontiacs, and trailing boozy husbands to their unholy nests. But it was a private life and I made my own hours. When it got hot and dead still, I felt bad about Linda. But not much.

# TWO

My office edges up against downtown, an area of mom-and-pop shops, hardware and shoe stores, lawn and garden emporiums, and the always-empty beauty parlor. There are vacant lots full of weeds, tin cans, discarded tires, and leftover houses with tumbled porches and dirt yards, old couples out front in the swing, all cancer and Social Security and no place to go. I like Lincoln Street though, elm-shaded and red-brick. I'm the end suite of three in a single-story, mud-colored row of offices set back off the street. Two blocks east on Lincoln looms Thomas Jefferson Elementary, built in 1929—stately, made of red brick like the street, a spidery silver fire escape trailing around the pointed roof and on down between the rows of tall, shimmering windows. In autumn, when the air sharpened and the elms glistened red and orange, I often contemplated the shining school windows, imagining paste and erasers and chalk smelling just as enviably fresh and clean as linen or apples. It was good then, or in early spring on a blustery

10

mid-morning in March, blue and gray clouds bumping along in the chilly air, to stroll the long block west down Lincoln to Betty's Coffee Pot, and there, in the white neon glare, to drink coffee and eat warm cinnamon rolls. I had the time these days and I was trying to be quiet, to gain something from being small and paying attention to detail.

I was next door to Jake Singleton's barbershop. Jake's nose looked like a roadmap of the Weller's distillery and he was the only guy I ever saw who really had Popeye forearms. "Bowling and jerking off," he told me, "and hell, that's what happens when yer damn dick weighs sixteen pounds." Jake cut my hair every two weeks, cigar ash and grayish-brown hair disappearing down my collar. He talked and I read *Field and Stream.* We both worried a lot about the rent on our places and I generally agreed with him that the potholes in the gravel parking lot were worse than ever this year. Jake said he wanted to try his concoction of HA Hair Arranger and lilac water on my head. "What the hell, HA finds out about this, we make a million." I liked Jake and he liked me, though he said he could never figure how a snoop could make an honest living.

It was the snipe end of a weary August, ten o'clock in the morning, when I skidded the Fairlane to a stop in front of the plate-glass window: MITCH ROBERTS INVESTIGATIONS. No staring eye or deerstalker hat, just a come in and venetian blinds. I waved at Jake and flashed him a grin. He was patiently cutting the hair of a fat guy who hardly had any, carressing the few strands of pasted-down black hair around the guy's crown, tilting his shiny head gently back and forth with steady hands, generally making the guy think he was really getting a haircut. For the bald guy it was like having a smart, good-looking whore ask to feel his muscles. A buck and a quarter and he got to hear what Jake had to say, read his *Field and Stream,* and look at the girl's ass on the calendar. Jake stuck his scissors in the pocket of his smock and returned a salute.

It was going to be hot again. In powdery sunlight, I

opened the office door and walked past Gertie's desk,
around the wood-and-glass divider, and sat down behind
the oak desk I got at Razook Furniture for $12.50. Gertie
would be late again, home with female trouble, or maybe
just weary and demoralized from my last shoot-out in the
office. Maybe she was out on an undercover assignment
for the boss. Hell, it didn't matter. Gertie had been born
two years before, when I went to the Kress store downtown
and bought a suede purse in blue, a cherry lipstick and
powder kit, and a three-by-five picture frame. I left the
paper photograph of Donald O'Connor in the picture frame
and set the stuff in a lifelike disarray. My regular clients—
the junior bank managers, the half dozen lawyers, the
handful of insurance adjusters—were mostly beyond kidding me about Gertie and her Donald O'Connor look-alike
husband. As for the rest, what few there were, I hoped they
would become regular clients before they found out I didn't
have a secretary and never would. Gertie saved me a lot of
shit.

I made some coffee on the hot plate and leafed through
title documents to my repossessions. One guy owned a
Hudson Hornet. I mean he and the bank owned the Hornet.
He had bought the thing two years ago and was now three
months shy on the payments, and the bank was feeling
insecure. The slob worked the last shift at Boeing, so he
got home about an hour after daybreak and probably started
drinking whiskey, chasing it with beer. I figured he was on
the run from the wife and kids, but couldn't get away from
the job that quick because he needed the dough. I also
figured that by ten he would be asleep on the couch in his
dirty efficiency at the Matthewson Apartments, bundled in
a white T-shirt with burp stains on the belly, a copy of
*Modern Detective* straddling his broken-down face. I had
to think about the guy that way. If I thought long enough
about the eight hours this guy spent burring rough edges
from metal pieces down at the plant, his wife's mother-in-
law on the back porch chewing tobacco, and the radio

blaring Don McNeil's *Breakfast Club* at eight in the morning when he was trying to sleep, I would think about tipping the guy to scram. Hanging on the way I was, I couldn't afford social theory. To me it was an easy daytime snatch, the owner dead on the couch. No guns, no fights, no hollering.

I was still matching car keys and title documents when the phone rang.

I answered in a tough-guy voice, adding a little: *My secretary didn't show this morning and I'm annoyed about that.* "Mitch Roberts."

The voice on the other end was Okie, about twenty years out of the hog thicket, slow and drooling, with an undertow of calculation. It was an ole-boy voice backed up by a little money.

"This here the private investigator?" This voice was definitely connected with a sneer. I could picture this voice shooting neighbor dogs, maybe setting a barn fire.

"Speaking," I said.

The voice said, "This here is Carl Plummer." I never heard of Carl Plummer, but the voice presumed I had. I decided to call the voice *Mr.* Plummer, see what happened and whether I was going to get some of that money.

"Well, Mr. Plummer, what can I do for you?"

"Do you find people? People who up and run off?"

"Mr. Plummer," I said, "I go and look for people who run off and sometimes I find them. Sometimes I don't."

"I say you do your job kinda half-assed then, boy." There was nothing in the tone to make me think I was being kidded.

"What's on your mind, Mr. Plummer?"

"I got a job fer you."

"If I take it."

"You can afford to sit around there with yer feet up waiting fer yer rich uncle to get his head sucked into the mowin' machine?"

"Mr. Plummer, I'd like to dance this two-step with you

for most of the rest of the night, but the widda Jones and her scrawny sisters are waiting out at the Tucker place for their bull. Now why don't we get down to business before my new blue seersucker suit plumb melts away?" I didn't trust the voice and I didn't like the Mr. Plummer it said it was, but so far this conversation was more fun than going over title documents with the junior assistant manager for credit compliance at Union National.

Mr. Plummer said, "Boy, you think you can find South Broadway?"

"I got a compass, a sack of sandwiches, and the Boy Scout Handbook right out in the car. It might take a week, but I'll find it." South Broadway was the main truck drag running north and south through Wichita. On Mr. Plummer's end, Broadway was Highway 81 running down to Oklahoma City and Dallas.

"Well now," Plummer said, "why don't you make a run at my place this afternoon. We'll see if you make er. I got some business where I need someone who can nose my son down. You shape up right to me, we might make some kinda deal." I knew being specific was not trump to an Okie no matter how long he was out of the hog thicket. "You know my place? Salvage yard down across the bridge."

"I'll find it, Mr. Plummer."

"I hope so. I surely de do hope so." He hung up.

I leaned back and lit a Lucky. I flipped the Yellow Pages through until I found "Salvage." Plummer's Salvage Yard was at Broadway and Thirty-ninth Street South, no high-priced ad, no slogan, no picture of a tow truck, just the name and phone number. I dialed the number. Plummer answered, "Salvage." And I hung up.

I dialed Andy Lanham. Andy was the lieutenant of detectives down at the WPD, a friend, and good for pulling license tags and running spot checks in return for french-fried cauliflower and a night at the ballpark. Sometimes Andy dropped by my place on Sycamore and we would sit beside the open window, play chess, and drink beer. Since the birth of his third kid, Andy dropped by less. We hadn't been to the ballpark together all summer. I was on hold at the switchboard for a minute, then Andy picked up his phone and said hello.

"Hello, Andy. How the heck are you?"

"Great, Mitch. Good to hear from you. You playing any chess these days? Those fucking Braves."

"Yes—and those Braves are the greatest." I was following the Botvinnik and Smyslov championship match pretty closely, at least until I got a little drunk in the evening and walked over to the park to watch the Braves for five innings. I lived across the street from Lawrence Stadium where the Braves played Triple-A ball.

"What can I do for you, Mitch?"

"Listen, Andy, I need a short favor."

"Shoot."

"Are you guys working any missing-persons case on a kid named Plummer? Don't know the first name. If so, what kind of action? Second, you got any record on Carl Plummer—arrests anywhere, any other beefs?"

Andy said, "Hold on. I'll be back." I lit another Lucky and waited.

Five minutes later Andy came back on the line. "No open case on any Plummer missing person. Also no reports. No arrests, wants, or beefs on Carl Plummer." I heard him drag a cigarette. In a sharp, serious way he added, "What's the action Mitch? You gone inquisitive?"

"Thanks a million, Andy. Drop by soon and we'll catch Indianapolis and play over some old Alekhine games."

Andy eased, disappointed. "Take it easy Mitch." He hung up.

I hung the BACK AT FIVE O'CLOCK sign on the glass door, put the top down on the Fairlane, and drove east on Lincoln through a cavern of dusty elms. I had done some missing-persons work in the past, mostly teenagers on a toot. Those were cases the police worked on, but the client was willing to spring the thirty-five a day for personal service. Three times a year I went looking for Mrs. Richard Donahue, whose idea of a really good time was a shack job in Kansas City with an ex-con or truck driver. Mr. Richard Donahue paid me fifty a day and left the police out.

Something bothered me about Carl Plummer and his missing son. There was no police beef, no missing money, no hint of alarm in Carl Plummer's voice. If anything, Plummer was mad as hell. I pulled up in a bus stop in front of the Uptown Recreation and hopped out. If there was anything out on the streets about Plummer, the Gar—bartender and small-time grifter—would know.

The decorator who appointed the Wreck was fond of sepia and blue neon. Saloon bar in front backed by a mirror, line of booths along one wall, and four snooker tables to the back door. Beaming, Tony Garcia stood with both hands on the bar. Above his head the Hamm's bear kept hitting a lighted golf ball over a forest and into a placid mountain lake.

"Roberts. Starting kinda early?"

"No thanks, Tony. How about some coffee?"

At the back snooker table two gas-and-electric guys clicked snooker balls around a perfect green felt table. They belonged to the G & E truck parked on Douglas. Taking a break.

"Sure thing. Just a minute," he said.

Tony owed me. One Saturday night I shot a fat woman in the foot. The fat woman had a butcher's knife in the Gar's belly and was about to butterfly his spleen. The Gar went down for two months, but he wasn't out.

Tony came out of the back room with my coffee. "So, Mitch," he said, "it is not Saturday night, there is no loose girls at the bar, you are wearing a suit. You are wanting information." Tony was doing Joel Cairo.

"Tony, you are a very wise man." I sipped the coffee. My eyes were getting used to the dark. Tony was a huge man with olive skin and black hair. His face was round, his left eye a sightless white. A rainbow scar ran from the corner of his white eye to his mouth.

"Does the name Carl Plummer mean anything to you, Tony?" I asked.

He looked over my shoulder at the pinball machine. "Carl Plummer. No, Mitch, it means nothing to me."

"Ask around a little for me would you, Tony? It is not an unimportant matter. Also, it would be best if it was not known that I am interested."

Tony laughed. "The word is as good as out."

I finished my coffee and left Tony with a promise to be back Saturday night for some snooker. The G & E guys were still on break when I hopped into the Fairlane and drove south on Hillside, like always, sticking to the shady tunnels on Wichita's old brick streets.

I spent a couple of hours doing my repos. The Hudson Hornet showed forty thousand miles and a ripped headliner, all in two years. The junior assistant manager for credit compliance was not amused with his collateral. After a Nu-Way burger, bowl of chili with onions, and a glass of beer, I was ready to go dancing with Carl Plummer.

South Broadway is the crawl space of Wichita. Hill people from Arkansas and Oklahoma, Ma and Pa and four or five kids jammed into broken-down jalopies, come north looking for jobs at aircraft plants, packing houses, or refineries. They make it to South Broadway. They are all along there, sitting on buckets and stumps in front of the Moon Motel, rooming by the week in hot little cubicles, the vacant-eyed scruffy kids throwing rocks at stray dogs. The street is littered with used-car lots, salvage yards, greasy spoons, and nightclubs. Every Sunday morning in the back pages of the *Eagle* you read about the guy kicked, stabbed, or shot to death in the parking lot of Cal's Lightning Lounge. It just means some hill family goes home to the hills without Pa.

I worked a lot of skip chases along there, sometimes Honest Al, other times Buck's. It happened that Honest Al used more oily sawdust in his transmissions than most, which meant that when I found the guy who owed Al money I towed the man and the car both. It was unpleasant work.

I drove across the WPA bridge over the Arkansas River, through the intersection at Twenty-ninth Street and past Honest Al's. Carl Plummer's salvage yard was on the right, surrounded on three sides by a ramshackle corrugated-metal fence, the back boundary the river levee. Five or six old cottonwoods with great gnarled trunks shaded the heaps of rusted wrecks, and seedpods filled the air with cotton balls. Dust enveloped the Ford.

When I pulled off the brick street I was in sand and loose dirt three inches deep, fine and silty. I drove through a portal of rusted truck frames and into a fiery wilderness of wrecked cars and trucks, windows smashed, seats torn out. Under one of the cottonwoods squatted a tar-paper shack about fifteen feet square, the walls covered with hubcaps, a sign over the screen door saying OFFICE. I parked, and thought about how long it was going to take to get my white oxfords white again.

A yellow mongrel lay in a wet, sandy hole by the screen door. He arched his back. Without lifting his head, the mutt curled his lips over a row of sharp teeth and let out a constant, unsettling growl, low and mean.

A voice called, "Who is that?" It was Plummer.

"Mitch Roberts."

Plummer snapped, "Abraham!" The dog stopped his growl. I opened the screen and went in.

Plummer sat behind a metal desk, picking his teeth with a small pocketknife. He was wiry, and from what I could see he was tall. His long arms were muscled and brown from working in the sun. Short sandy hair, narrow eyes and a gray, shaggy beard—he looked leathery and lean. He didn't move when I came in, just sat in the wind from a fan stuck in a window behind him.

"Mr. Plummer."

"You eat all yer sandwiches?"

"Not quite." I wondered if the patter was permanent.

"You want the job looking for my boy?"

"That depends," I said.

Plummer looked up. He folded the knife slowly and put it in his pocket. "Depends on what?"

I was standing. There were no chairs in the shack. The whole greasy place was filled with generators, radios, drive shafts. "Now why don't you tell me what you want and why? Then I'll tell you whether it's possible, and if it is whether or not I'll do it for you. If I say it's possible and I'll do it for you, then we'll talk about how much you're going to pay me and when. Then if I agree to the arrangement I'll get to work. Up to now, Mr. Plummer, I don't like the dance and I don't think much of my partner. That's how it is." Plummer leaned back.

"All right," he said. He was smiling now, but it was sinister. "It's like this. My boy is Frank. Frankie Plummer. He's been gone three, four days. Supposed to be working for me around here. What I want is that you go looking for him, find him, and bring him back here. Put him in a goddamn basket if you have to. The why is—he just run off. That's all."

"Why don't you go find him yourself?"

"I ain't got the time."

"How old is he?"

"Old enough." In the corner of my eye I saw a figure outside the screen, just standing.

"Well, Mr. Plummer," I said, "If he's old enough, then he's entitled to leave home and not be dragged back. Suppose, if I go looking for him and find him, that I just tell you where he is and you can take your own basket and bring him back. Kidnapping is a beef I don't need."

Plummer thought for a moment. "All right," he said again.

"I need something to go on," I said, "like photographs of Frankie, some idea of his friends, a line on his car, where he hangs out, what kind of money he has. If he drinks, I want to know where. If he's fucking someone, I want to know who." Plummer was getting mad. I went on. "I get fifty a day and reasonable expenses."

Plummer didn't like any of this. His ears reddened. "I get yer picture," he said. "Frankie has money, he drives a blue '55 Pontiac. He don't stick to one bar more'n another, he ain't got no friends." Empty silence. Lower now. "You try talking to someone named Carmen Granger, lives up in Riverside. She may tell you something." Plummer nodded at the figure at the screen door. He went on. "Frankie stays down at that trailer on the levee. There's a picture from his high school in there somewhere, probably the desk drawer. I'll pay the fifty."

I didn't flinch at the name Carmen Granger. "I'll work for you, Mr. Plummer. Give me a few days. If I don't turn anything, I'll let you know and get off. If I do, you'll hear from me." I turned, then looked back. "Frankie ever been in trouble with the police?"

Plummer said, "No." He barked. "Gomez! Take Mr. Roberts down to the trailer." For the first time, he put his blue eyes directly in mine. "You be in touch. You try Carmen Granger and you be in touch. I expect that." Carl Plummer was making certain where I started.

It turns out Gomez was the lurker at the screen door, a dark-eyed punk about twenty, greasy and trying to act tough. He wore overalls with the name "Tomas" over the heart. Gomez was trying to grow a mustache, but for now it was just a few black hairs looking very lonely above his lip.

"This way," he said. I followed Gomez through the wreckage and back to the levee where the small, twelve-foot travel trailer was parked. It had seen better days. I looked at the ground around the trailer. There were no tire tracks, no oil spots. The trailer stood in direct sunlight, surely over ninety-five. I was thinking that if I lived in a tin can I would park it in the shade. I would also park my car next door. Gomez stood aside and I stepped up on a cinder block and went inside.

It was an airless oven. There were dishes in the little aluminum sink and a calendar on the wall. No phone. I walked to the rear and saw that the bunk bed was unmade. I looked inside the tiny closet. It was empty. Gomez stuck his head inside and said, "Come on. The picture is in that drawer." He pointed to the counter next to the sink.

I opened the drawer Gomez pointed to. In a mess of rags, tools, kitchen utensils, and matches, Frankie Plummer stared up. The picture had been scissored out of a yearbook. The kid looked a lot like his father. I reached with my left hand and casually turned the cold-water tap. Nothing. Gomez snapped, "What you doing, man? Come on." I went outside.

I held the picture up to Gomez. "Is this Frankie Plummer?"

"Yeah."

"How long ago?"

"Five, maybe six years."

"He change anything?"

"Hair's longer. That's all. Kind of ducktail. You know." That made Frankie twenty-three and pretty. But he didn't live in any trailer down by the levee at the junkyard. He had money and drove a new blue Pontiac. Carmen Granger knew where he might be. Frankie just didn't sound like a hill boy with his thumb up his ass.

Gomez followed me all the way to my car, saying nothing. I got in and started the engine. "So long, sonny," I said and smiled. Gomez was saying something, but I was already pulling away, digging through sand, gunning the engine.

I was in traffic, settled behind a Texaco tanker. I lit a Lucky and took a deep drag, thinking. Carl Plummer was not a fool, so he would never expect me to believe that he was just a worried old dad missing his sweet little boy. For some reason he wanted me to believe that Frankie lived in the trailer down by the levee, but didn't have the time or savvy to make it look convincing. Carl also wanted me to think that Frankie boy broke down front ends and scrounged parts. Maybe he did. But it didn't seem likely somehow. What got me was the part about Carmen Granger, Carl tossing off her name like it was supposed to be nothing, just another girlfriend. Hell.

I got under the shady elms on Harry Street and went west.

In the green, cool mountains of north Pakistan, brown bears abound. Natives from Lahore go up to the foothills in summer, stun a little bear out of his tree with a rock or club, stick a ring through his wet nose, and cart him down to steamy, tropical Lahore. You see the bears all over there, matted scabrous skin, watery eyes, dancing in endless circles, standing on hind legs in garbage, surrounded by a laughing mass of toothless, turbaned people. The little bears bleed from their paws. They live five or six years.

I got thirty-five a day, but if Carl Plummer was willing to pay fifty, he could have me for a while. I could feel the ring, hear the toothless laughter.

# THREE

It was almost five when I got back to the office. Jake was closed, already home with his wife, Katherine, TV blaring Deputy Dusty and the grill boiling charcoal. There was a letter waiting for me from Jack Graybul, one of the half-dozen shysters who sometimes spoon me work. Jack laconically offered one of those take-it-or-leave-it, twenty-dollar-a-day "injury scouts" he sometimes got the insurance company to spring. It seems some poor bastard was riding his kid's pogo stick down the basement stairs, showing off, when the thing fell apart and sent the guy bouncing down the steps on his forehead and eyebrows. The guy claimed he couldn't walk, talk, or fuck, and was suing Duckwall's five-and-dime, Mattel Toys, a metal manufacturer in New Jersey, and J. Edgar Hoover for fifty million bucks. Graybul wanted me to hang around the guy's house for a couple of days to see if the aggrieved party started doing hundred-yard dashes. If he did, I got fifty for testifying. Graybul was not beyond offering me three hundred for testifying anyway, but he did it half-hearted.

Graybul was the kind of guy who smoked constantly and had bad dandruff: his cheap serge suits looked polka-dotted. He French-inhaled without taking the cigarette out of his mouth, and could argue a case and eat lunch that way too. Once another shyster hired me to tail Graybul around town on an adultery caper filed by his wife. It turned out he was seeing a cashier at Brown's Grill on Central Street across from the hospital. She had braces on her legs from having polio. Jack would see her sometimes at lunch hour, buy her a gardenia at the flower shop next door, and then they would go across to a little park and sit and talk and look at the tulips. Jack never touched her except to kiss her cheek. I turned in a report giving Jack a clean bill of health and never bothered to find out whether he stayed with her at night or not.

Jack loves the trumpet. He sits for hours in his eighth-floor office facing a blank brick wall, playing flourishes and trills. When I give my reports to him he plays while I talk, making the song fit the report. The time I recovered a stolen Persian cat for an old lady out in Eastborough, Jack played "Hold That Tiger," wrote out my fifty-buck check, and never missed a beat. His secretary was going nuts, and Jack was going broke. He was tawdry and tired, but he always paid on time even if it killed him at home. I figured to be finished with Plummer in a couple of days and decided to call Jack Monday morning and start earning my twenty a day watching some guy force himself to hobble around.

I walked through the office, pulled a Pabst out of the refrigerator in the storeroom, and went through the back door. I sat in my rocker and rocked under a mimosa tree, cracked the beer, and lit a smoke. Somewhere behind me the sun was setting, sending dusty rays of orange and gold through the mimosa flowers, lighting the green elms that

swayed in the breeze. It was getting cooler. Heat lightning-
showed on the prairie to the north of town and thunder-
heads, black and yellow and purple, were building far
away. It smelled like rain.

I couldn't figure out the part about Carmen Granger and
Frankie-boy Plummer. If Carl wanted Frankie to marry or
fuck his way into money, he couldn't do better than Carmen Granger, and from what I heard, she was a knockout
to boot. So it figured that Carl didn't want me to put
Frankie in a basket. What he probably wanted was to find
out what was going on and how. But I didn't have a clue as
to why. I finished the beer and the cigarette and decided to
stake out the Granger house in Riverside. It's better to cop
a feel of the merchandise before buying. I locked up and
drove home.

I live on Sycamore in the bottom half of an old shingle
house. I've got two big rooms and a walk-in kitchen, brass
doorknobs, and a stained-glass window through to the
backyard. Mrs. Thompson lives upstairs with her cat,
Francis, and parakeet, Tweeter. Francis sits all day and
stares at Tweeter while Mrs. Thompson listens to the radio.
She is real quiet. Once in a while she shuffles downstairs in
her tattered housecoat to ask what day it is in case her son
is coming with the week's groceries or to take her to the
doctor. Mrs. Thompson thinks I'm a real nice young man
because I don't make noise and chase women. I don't
know what she thinks about the boxes and sacks full of
muscatel bottles.

All I own in the world is in the apartment: rolltop desk,
teak Staunton chess set, brass bed and Grandma's quilt,
two Hopper prints, a set of Hegel, one 9mm Browning
automatic. I thought of buying an air cooler, but couldn't
bring myself to do it. I decided to save a dollar a week for
a bamboo fly rod and I had fifty bucks squirreled in a pair
of brogues. I kept figuring that in another two years I
would have the fly rod, but every time I looked in the Bean

catalogue the price went up thirty dollars. It looked like I
would be casting for Dolly Varden from a wheelchair at the
old folks' home.

I parked the Ford around back in a shed beside the
neighbors' chicken coop and scuffled my way through the
fallen catalpa beans to the front porch. Francis was perched
on one of the eaves above, watching while I got the mail
out of the box on the wall. The mail was a cardboard roll
from England, the poster-size photograph of Carl
Schlecter, one of my heroes—a pale, callow ghost with
piercing black eyes and disheveled hair. Schlecter played
the great Lasker for the world chess championship in Ber-
lin, 1910. In the twentieth and last game Schlecter led
Lasker by a full game and needed only a draw to become
champion at age twenty-one. He played ruthlessly, and
midway through the game had a winning position. Most of
the burghers in that baroque pavilion thought Schlecter
would encase himself in an impregnable shell, play cau-
tiously, and lock up the championship. Schlecter attacked.
He remained himself. The wily Lasker defended patiently,
then ensnared Schlecter in an invisible iron net. Finally,
Schlecter resigned. The match was drawn, and Lasker re-
tained his championship. Four years later Schlecter died of
starvation that first cold winter of World War I. There was
something romantic and sad and courageous in all that and,
except for baseball, life didn't seem to offer much in the
way of romance and courage. So I added Carl Schlecter to
the Hopper prints.

I stripped to my shorts and poured a tall muscatel with
ice cubes. I got out a piece of veal, pounded on it for a
while with a serrated hammer, breaded it, and stuck it in
the ice box. Then I made a big salad, adding a couple of
tomatoes from my plot out in the backyard. I heated a pan
of peanut oil and dropped the veal into it. I made gravy
from bacon grease, flour, and milk, and added a little
lemon juice. By the time I was ready to eat I had downed
three glasses of muscatel, the fireflies were making circles

in the quiet evening air, and the heat lightning was coming closer to town.

I ate dinner, my feet propped in the front window. I looked through my toes over the left-field wall of the ball-park, past two rows of orange boxcars, to the slow Arkansas River and downtown, twinkling in the hazy twilight. As I sopped the last tomato in olive oil and lemon, a dusty blue Plymouth pulled up in front. Andy Lanham, smoking a cigar, got out, waved, and walked through the shadows and fireflies to the front porch.

Andy was all angles and bones, the kind of fellow you call "Red" when you're a kid. He came into the house smiling and said, "Hello, Mitch. I figured it was about time to drink a beer and try out a new opening. Your phone call reminded me that we hadn't played for a while. What the hell, you up for it?" The Dutch Masters he puffed smelled like a wet dog. I lit a Lucky and puffed back.

"Andy," I said, "my heart goes out to the cops, eternally clad in wrinkled suits and serving the undeserving public. How are you?"

"Fine, Mitch, really fine. When the public is as slovenly and hopeless as you, this job is a pain in the ass." He saw Schlecter on the wall over my rolltop. "Ah, Schlecter." There seemed nothing more to say.

"What has the lieutenant been working on lately?"

"You know, Mitch, the usual. Two guys are drinking beer and shooting pool down on South Broadway. Someone starts to lose and things get nasty. Out in the parking lot a .22 comes out and one guy gets gut-shot, takes him thirty minutes to fucking die. The uniformeds show first, later Andy Lanham interviews witnesses, and it takes an hour to straighten everybody out. The crime is solved. Everybody but the dead guy goes home." Andy shook his head and shrugged.

"You mean you don't get too many hound of the Baskerville murders with a dollop of gold bug capers?"

"You got it. It's just three yards and a cloud of dust."

"Well," I said, "sit." Andy took off his wrinkled jacket and showed me the blue knit shirt with sweat rings around the underarms. He wore a shoulder holster and a police special. He looked tired as hell.

"How about a beer, a game of chess, and some decent conversation?"

"That's fine," Andy said, "just fine." I went to the refrigerator and got a can of Pabst, pulled the Staunton board to the window, and handed the beer to Andy. He was quiet, setting up his pieces. I thought he was nervous, kind of fidgety. He chose white.

We played for a while; then, when I asked him how things were going at home, he told me about his new kid. Andy wasn't saying much, just sitting hunched over and tired-looking in the open window. I tried talking about Eisenhower, about the Braves, about the gob of pigeon shit on the hood of the Fairlane. Nothing moved him, and so after a while I just sat quietly drinking muscatel and playing chess. I used a Caro-Kann to his king-pawn opening, a strategy I new fairly well from following Botvinnik in the latest championship matches. Andy was a good player, but tonight his moves were disconnected and pointless. After ten moves he was down a pawn with no development and no organization.

Andy sat crouched over, his head in his hands. He asked quietly, "You been working on anything special lately?"

"Nothing special."

"Anything going down on your search for Frankie Plummer?"

"Nothing yet."

"Say, who is this guy Plummer anyway? You were pretty tight-lipped about it. It sounds interesting." Andy studied the board, then moved a knight he had moved before, wasting tempo.

"I told you," I said. "He may be missing. I'm not sure yet." Andy had let his cigar go out. "How about another beer, Andy?" He told me thanks but no and made an aim-

less pawn move. I cleared out the black squares for my
bishop and doubled rooks on the knight file against his
king. Andy turned and looked out the window. Thunder
rumbled far away.

"It must be good to get something meaty for a change,
instead of repos and that stuff, huh?" he said. "I mean, a
real live missing person out of the textbooks. What is the
first move on a deal like this anyway?" There was no con-
viction in his voice. He picked up his cigar and stuffed the
wet, chewed end in his mouth. I drank some muscatel. I
was thinking about a knight sacrifice on the bishop file. I
said nothing, letting the silence and the distant thunder
build.

Andy was getting more nervous. "Huh?" he said. "You
gonna just go out and start looking for this kid Plummer
from scratch? You got any leads?"

I took a large slug of muscatel and with my right hand
swept all the pieces to the side of the board. The game was
over. "What the fuck is this? What the fuck is going on?" I
thought I sounded angry. "You come around here and expect me to spill my guts about Carl Plummer and Frankie-
boy. You called him Frankie. I never said anything about
that. What the hell? You drop by on Friday night about
seven just to play some chess and drink beer? Is that it?
Bullshit! If you're off duty, then you go home and put a kid
on each knee and play pablum patsy, you talk to the wife,
maybe watch the fights. Mow the fucking lawn. You don't
come over here and play chess and drink beer. If you're on
the clock, then what the fuck do you want with me and
why are you nosing around? I don't like it, so tell me or get
the hell out."

Andy was looking at me now, his face scarlet. He said
nothing.

"Well?" I waited. "My guess is Bull Granger pulled the
puppet string and sent old Andy over to find out what I
know. What I don't know is why. But if Colonel Granger
says stick a hot poker up your friend's ass, Lanham, then

you stick a hot poker up my ass and go back and report.
So, you got Colonel Granger and his little daughter Carmen to look out for. And me—I got a poker up my ass."

"I'm sorry you feel that way, Mitch."

"What's the answer, Andy? Did Bull Granger send you
here?"

Andy stood up and put on his jacket. "I'll be going," he
said, turned, walked out the door and through the gathering
night to his unmarked Plymouth. He paused, then got in
and drove away.

It was hard to figure why a hill man like Carl Plummer
would spring fifty a day to have me check up on his son
Frankie, especially since the kid was sniffing the pants leg
of someone like Carmen Granger. It was even harder to
figure why old Bull Granger, Mr. W. P. Granger—colonel
in the Wichita Police Department, head of Vice, adviser to
the Chief—would assign a lieutenant to ferret information
out of a small-time gumshoe like me. If Bull Granger
didn't like the idea of Frankie Plummer running his daughter, then the Bull Granger I had read about would waddle
up to Frankie Plummer and break his arm. Nothing ex-
plained why Granger would send Andy Lanham over here.
I knew Andy well enough to know that he was busted up
about doing it, and that hangdog look on his face when he
turned and drove off proved it. So I was stuck with a police
colonel and a junk hill man both interested in Frankie
Plummer, but not able to walk right up to him and lay their
cards on the table. To me, that meant that Frankie Plummer
had something on these two clowns besides an interest in
Carmen Granger. But if Frankie Plummer had something
besides Carmen Granger, how did she fit in?

There was one thing I knew. I'd made a mistake talking
to Andy that way. The story of my blowup was going to get
back to Bull Granger sooner or later. I should have played
dumb. Muscatel and friendship had got in the way of my
judgment.

A cool east wind blew the catalpas and elms around

outside the front windows. Night crickets clattered. I
laughed softly at myself, at how smart and tough I believed
I was, realizing I had made a beginner's mistake. It was
like the time at Carlsbad in 1929 when Nimzowitch lost a
game to a *patzer,* jumped on his chair in the quiet tourna-
ment hall, and fired a heavily weighted rook through an
open window. He shouted, "How can I lose to such a
fool?" Nimzowitch and I should have kept quiet. The way
it was, I might as well have sent a telegram to Bull
Granger.

By the time I finished the muscatel and a last cigarette it
was after ten. I took a cool shower and dressed in jeans,
flannel shirt, Red Wing boots, and windbreaker. I got a
rain hat out of my chest of drawers and put a fancy blackjack in my back pocket. I took thirty dollars out of my
wallet, put the wallet under my pillow, then put the thirty
dollars and my investigator's license in the heel of my left
boot. I locked up and went out to the Fairlane and put the
top up. The night was dark. Arcturus glimmered pale red
on the black horizon and a misty wedge of moon hovered
in the cottonwood along the riverbank. I could smell fall in
the air. I remembered that tomorrow it would be September.

Carmen Granger lived on Nims across from Riverside
Park and the zoo. I drove down Central in the fog, across
the river, then circled the park. I parked in dense shadow
by the Murdock Bridge. The three-story gabled place she
lived in was two hundred yards away, obscured by elms
and cottonwoods and the lion house. It was one of those
Victorian gingerbreads, porch wrapped around three sides,
carriage house, and gazebo, all on a corner lot surrounded
by a black iron fence. Abbott and Costello met the Wolf
Man in a house like that. I took my binoculars from the
glove box and strung them around my neck. I walked
slowly through the park, looking for a perch.

I found a wooden bench in the dark near the open-air
bear exhibit. The bears had a rock pile and swimming

hole, but they mostly slept and ate and swatted flies. They moved around more than the alligators, but not much. Owl hoots. Two macaws conducted an auction. I sat in the dark, fired up a Lucky, and waited. I had a half-pint of Old Overholt and hit it. There was no porch light at the Granger house, but a dim glow showed in the main room downstairs. I saw a white stripe on the grounds of the house where a night-light burned in the pantry. There was no motion. Maybe the people were asleep. I smoked, drank rye whiskey, and traded winks with an ostrich.

An hour went by, then two. At midnight a blue Pontiac roared over the bridge on Nims, pulled into the driveway of the Granger house, and stopped. A woman got out, opened the carriage-house door, returned to the Pontiac, then drove the big car into the dark shed. Through the binoculars I watched her walk up the porch steps and disappear through the front door and into the dim interior. The door shut. I was pretty sure it was Carmen Granger. She was tall and slim and wore a white pants suit, light gray raincoat. From what I could see in the foggy night she had a terrific figure; she walked erect, swiftly, holding an umbrella. She wore a straw panama. I thought she was smoking, but I couldn't be sure. One thing I was sure of: the car Carmen Granger drove was a '55 Pontiac, blue, clean, and in tune, a car that belonged to Frankie Plummer, at least according to Carl Plummer. I sat tight. In an hour the Overholt and Luckys would be gone and maybe I would have earned fifty bucks.

Behind me the bears snored dully. Then on the path leading through the trees to Nims two figures appeared, walking briskly my way. Both wore trenchcoats and felt hats. The guy on the left was built like a coal barge—thick neck, heavy occipital ridges, and bushy eyebrows. His buddy was shorter, left hand hidden in his coat pocket. It looked to me like these goons were trolling for shit and I was a turd. There was no use running, and after the Overholt I didn't feel like it anyway.

Coal Barge and his buddy got close enough to let their thick shadows fall either side of me on the bench.

"Looks like we got us a bird-watcher," Coal Barge said. The binoculars around my neck weighed fifty pounds.

Buddy put his other hand in his pocket. "The queers are sucking dick over at the shelter in Oak Park. Or didn't you know?" he said. He snickered. I went to high school with these kinds of guys and now they were cops, using the same lines they used after study hall. Okay, I'll meet you after school kind of stuff. I could act tough, innocent, or scared. It was always better to act tough.

"Your parents know where you are?" I said.

"Funny." Coal Barge.

"Actually, I'm bird-watching. Looking for yellow-backed flatfeet. Travel in pairs. Late-nighters. They're called yellow-backed because they travel in pairs, but they're harmless really. Their call is the wisecrack." It was the whiskey talking, but me that was getting rousted.

Coal Barge took a step forward. Buddy put a hand on his arm. Buddy was in charge, and it was Buddy who I had to deal with.

"You have a date downtown, slick," Buddy said. "Get up." I had been downtown before.

"Suppose you tell me the beef," I said.

"Suppose we cut the crap," Buddy said, "or we'll put some of your teeth in our pockets. We can roll you downtown in a tin can or you can get the fuck up and come around like a good little man. Right now I don't give a goddamn. You got a choice."

"Gosh oh golly," I said, "since you put it like that I think I'll come along. Let's go."

Coal Barge looked disappointed. We walked in silence to the blue Plymouth parked on Nims, down the block from Carmen Granger's house. I was not surprised to see it after Andy's visit earlier. Coal Barge drove. Only one thing bothered me. Carrying a blackjack in Kansas was good for six months in the city jail. And when I got out I would be back at Fox-Vliet packing crates of streptomycin.

The Wichita Police Department occupied all six stories of a sandstone rococo palace downtown. The building looked like it was built by a mad Ludwig of the prairie—gables, cornices, archways, and clock tower. Inside, though, it had that dreary look all police departments dredge up out of a collective unconscious. The walls were green up to shoulder level, then puce. The place stank of disinfectant and sweat. In the distance someone was crying. My playmates and I went up the elevator to the third floor. A Negro woman sat on a metal chair outside the Bull's door, her nose bleeding. No one paid any attention at all.

Coal Barge opened the door and I saw Bull Granger sitting behind a gray metal desk. He was a big man with a sandy crew cut, a flat face, and a neck the size of a stovepipe. I could tell he was mad, because the veins in that neck stuck out like ropes. I counted his heart rate and it was high.

Coal Barge pulled a chair in front of the desk and said, "Sit down, scumbag." They didn't check the back pocket. I sat.

Bull spoke in a growl, his voice as flat as his face. "You tell me what you are doing outside my daughter's house. Then you tell me it won't happen again." Bull had that south Wichita drawl that bordered on a whine. Nasal and sharp.

"Well, Colonel, I tell ya. I've never seen ostriches fuck. They didn't tonight."

"Maybe you don't know it," the Bull said, "but Detective Sergeant Davis here is aching to put yer dick ina pencil sharpener. I'll see it happens, then I'll see you sit in jail till yer mother forgets you exist."

"You got a charge, Colonel?"

"We'll think of something."

"You better get busy thinking. It's not your strong suit."

The Bull got up and walked in front of the desk and sat

on the edge. He was about two feet in front of me. He smelled like Lysol and sweat and his heart rate was way up there. The Bull slapped me full across the face. I didn't move.

"You get it, fuckface. You're a little turd in a big cistern. What yer doing I want it stopped. Yer out of yer league. I won't tell you again. Leave my daughter alone. Don't hang around, don't peep. Call Carl Plummer and resign. You'll last longer." At least I knew I was right about Andy Lanham. He had been in to see the Bull about me. I still didn't know why.

I moved my feet apart. If this got worse I figured to kick Coal Barge in the knee and give myself fifteen seconds with the Bull. A blackjack can even things out real fast.

"Colonel," I said, "you mind telling me why?"

"Don't think. Crawl back into your slime hole. You get it?" I really didn't like the Bull.

"I get it," I said.

The Bull looked at Coal Barge. "Escort this fried peckerwood out to the street."

At the door I turned and looked back at the Bull, still sitting on the edge of his metal desk. He wore a rumpled blue suit with an American flag on the lapel.

"Colonel," I said, holding my voice down and calm, "you touch me again and you better kill me."

As I turned to leave he said, "You got a deal, peckerwood." I walked the two miles home and thought things over. It was a cinch I wouldn't give up on Frankie Plummer.

When I got home the eastern sky was pink and gold. The goddamn birds twittered wildly. My mouth tasted of Overholt and Luckys and my jaw hurt. I decided I had earned my fifty for that day.

# FOUR

Finally, the birds gave up their stupid twitter. I got a solid three hours of sleep.

Then Mrs. Thompson was pounding at my back door, as insistent as a seventy-six-year-old can get. A lovely morning.

"Mr. Mitch, Mr. Mitch!" Her voice was one part hysteria, one part simple panic. "Mr. Mitch, Mr. Mitch!" I loved being called Mr. Mitch, seeing myself in a Frank Capra movie about small-town America before things got complicated.

"I'll be right there, Mrs. Thompson," I shouted. It wouldn't do any good to shout at Mrs. Thompson. She could barely hear. But everybody shouts at deaf people. I wrapped myself in a dirty bathrobe and creaked to the back door. My jaw hurt, my ankles were stiff, and my eyes burned. On the way past the bathroom mirror I sneaked a look. I was not a pretty picture. Mrs. Thompson pounded and shouted, shouted and pounded. Everybody in the neighborhood was used to Mrs. Thompson except the Aleys next door who thought she was a witch. The Aleys also thought Truman was a Communist and Mitch Miller a musician.

I opened the back door and put a hand on Mrs. Thompson's quaking shoulder. She was wringing her hands. The cotton lining of her housecoat showed through the rips.

"Is my son coming today? Is my son coming today?" she screamed.

"What day do you expect him?" I shouted, then caught myself and picked up the pad and pencil on the counter by the sink. I wrote on the pad: WHAT DAY IS YOUR SON SUPPOSED TO COME?

Mrs. Thompson cradled the precious message in her trembling fingers, panicked, and shouted twice as loud as before. "Oh, is it today? I just can't remember!" I wrote on the pad again: WHAT DAY DID HE SAY HE WAS COMING? Mrs. Thompson thought a moment, still shaking. "Wednesday," she barked. I wrote TODAY IS ONLY SATURDAY, HE WILL COME IN FOUR DAYS.

Mrs. Thompson smiled sheepishly, feeling helpless and ashamed. I didn't like that part of our visits. I patted her on the back. From the pocket of her housecoat Mrs. Thompson pulled a scurrilous-looking apple and held it out to me. I mouthed "thank you" and accepted it. She turned and climbed the treacherous stairs to her place.

Well, I was up. I put some coffee on to perk and started a frying pan full of link sausage. I broke eggs into a bowl, added cinnamon and cream, then sopped three slices of bread in the egg. While the sausage and French toast and coffee cooked, I got the sports page of the *Eagle* and checked the scores. The Browns had left St. Louis for Baltimore, so now I followed the Cards. They always came in second or third, sometimes worse. Last night they beat the Cubbies, the McDaniel brothers pitching a combined seven-hitter, with Stan the Man cracking a game-winning double in the seventh. Phil Stevens was gone forever. He went down with his mike. But for an announcer the Cards had Harry Caray intoning his breathless, maniacal, "It might be, it could be, it might be, *it is. A home run!*" Myth transformed into magic. I'd have to miss the afternoon game from Chicago if I wanted to go have a talk with Carmen Granger. Colonel Bull or no Colonel Bull, there were fifty simoleons at stake. Besides, I hoped that broad daylight would make a difference to my night-creeping friends Coal Barge and Buddy.

I sat down with the coffee, sausages, and French toast. I poured Vermont maple syrup over the toast. My Grandpa Roberts sent me the syrup in one of those little souvenir packing crates, the only present he ever gave me. No one knew why he sent it and my Grandma Roberts was stunned. Then, two years ago, Grandma found Grandpa face down on a gravel road, stone dead from a heart attack. When I poured the syrup, I felt I was using up Grandpa's secret, trading the magic beans for a cow. When it was gone it would be gone forever. I ate the sausage and toast and thought about Grandpa Roberts.

Grandpa flimflammed his way through the 1930s. He found a farmhouse or a shack at the edge of a little Kansas hamlet, then disappeared for a year, maybe two. Grandpa also sold Bibles, which was legit. He sold magic pills, which was probably not. He talked to anybody who'd listen about flower gardens. "Them roses look a little punish," he'd say. Friends and neighbors would explain how they ordered the bushes from the catalogue and they came all dried up and limp and they put them in the ground and nothing was growing pretty. At that point, Grandpa would tell about a miracle pill he had that made roses—floribundas, hybrids, and all—grow strong and pretty and bloom twice a year. June and September.

"Now," Grandpa would say, "you put this pill in a bucket of water, dissolve it, and pour the water on the rosebush every third day during the summer. You water roses every third day and they're gonna bloom like a dang virgin at a barn dance."

But Grandpa made his real living cheating the big landowner, banker, and capitalist. He would put an advertisement in the local rag of some hick county seat—offering oil leases for sale to the highest bidder. Make it look official and important. In small print he stuck something about all sales subject to credit checks and cash deposits. That kind of thing appealed to folks, to their greed and vanity. Then he showed up in town a couple of days before the auction driving a swell car, acting all business and secrecy. Before long he had the local banker trying to jump the gun on the auction. Grandpa would hold out a long time, "setting the hook." He wasn't anxious to get involved in anything shady. The night before the auction, the banker would fairly force the money into Grandpa's pocket, and Grandpa would give him a frilly paper full of legalese, describing the leases and the rights of the parties. Then Grandpa would leave town—driving all night across the state line to Cherryvale to get drunk and look for a woman.

Finally, electricity and telephones came to almost all the farmhouses, run-down or not. The dirt roads turned to gravel, then asphalt, then became county roads and U.S. highways. Maybe the county clerks got smarter. They even put radios in the police cars. "There's just too goddamn much information," Grandpa said when they put him in Lansing for five years, drawling the word *information,* saying each syllable like a separate word. He was in the slammer for only two years. For eight years after that, Grandpa stayed home and cut hair in a barber chair out back on the porch of the farm. He didn't ever look very happy. Then one day Grandma found his corpse on the gravel road. Grandma got a barber chair, a tweed suit, a set of scissors and combs, and six sons and daughters. Me, I had half a jug of maple syrup.

After breakfast I took a long, cool shower. My heart started beating again so I decided it was time to deal the hand, to visit the Granger house. I wore my blue seer-sucker suit, white cotton shirt, pale blue tie with white puffy-cloud design, white oxfords, and a touch of Old Spice. I felt like a slave to a barbershop quartet. I copped a last look at myself in the mirror, wrapped some aviator sunglasses around my eyes to calm the sun, then stuck that fancy blackjack in my rear pocket to calm my nerves. I could get through the day imagining a blackjack looped hard up onto the septum of Bull Granger's nose.

I retrieved the Fairlane and drove up Sycamore to Douglas and went east across the Broadview Bridge into downtown. The sky sparkled clear and blue; the cold front that had moved through last night left the air clean and mild and ready for fall. It was a good day in Wichita. I turned north and parked next to the boathouse, about three blocks across the park and zoo from Carmen Granger's house.

I walked the shady side of Nims without bringing any gorillas out of the jungle. When the door opened, Carmen Granger froze me with her pale sapphire eyes. "Yes, what is it?"

She looked about twenty and wore a white cotton frock that set off her copper skin. On her feet were rope sandals. She smelled like the dew on a daffodil. I smelled like Old Spice and Lucky Strike Red.

"My name is Mitch Roberts. If you're Carmen Granger, I'd like to talk to you. It won't take long."

She stared at me with her sapphire eyes. She had a thin, young face and high cheekbones, pure black hair falling around her shoulders. The only makeup she had on was a touch of eye shadow and some peach lipstick. I wished I had big muscles and a tan.

"What is it you want?" she asked.

"I want to talk about Frankie Plummer." Behind her a staircase rose and abruptly disappeared into the second floor darkness. She stood in an entryway, sunlight pouring through a window on her left. I couldn't see the blue Pontiac anywhere in the drive, but a pink Thunderbird was parked by the carriage-house shed. I could also see the outline of Carmen Granger's body through her white frock. She stepped back slightly.

"I see," she said coolly. "In that case you had better come in."

Double mahogany doors opened onto the main room downstairs. It was large, airy, and high-ceilinged, a set of bay windows catching the light and green of the park. The parquet floors smelled of wax. A mug of yellow roses stood on a shiny black grand piano. Through one of the windows I saw a woman digging with a trowel in the garden. The yellow roses were her work.

"Please sit down," she said. "May I get you something to drink? Something cool?"

"Have you any Earl Grey with a sprig of fresh mint?" She laughed at that one, a nice small laugh, very authentic.

"I'm having gin and grapefruit juice, lots of ice. But I can get you a cup of instant Folger's if you like."

"Gin and grapefruit juice, then," I said. It was hard to see any Bull Granger in Carmen. She walked past me to the rear of the house, her sandals scraping the parquet.

"May I smoke?" I said.

Quietly: "Of course."

The kitchen and pantry were behind me. I could hear her humming softly to herself. I figured four rooms upstairs, probably bedrooms and a study or den, another attic bedroom above them. I smoked beside the fireplace and flicked ashes into it. I didn't see any ashtrays. I was tempted to open the drawers of a big desk in the corner, but fought it off. On the desk was a picture of a dark-haired woman with black, limpid eyes. She looked about fifty and wore a lace mantilla. Her face bore an expression of unbearable sadness. By the time Carmen came back into the big room carrying a silver tray and two drinks, I had finished my Lucky.

I sipped the gin and grapefruit juice.

"You have a lovely home," I said. One of Elgar's symphonies floated into the room. "I didn't think Elgar penetrated the prairie past Peoria."

She sipped her gin. "I don't want to be rude, Mr. Roberts, but you mentioned the name Frankie Plummer and said it would only take a minute. We are working on several minutes already."

"All right," I said. "A kid named Frank Plummer needs someone to find him. Me. I have reason to believe you know where he is. If you do, then you could help by telling me what you know."

"What is your interest in this matter?" She didn't sound rude or anxious, just businesslike and short. I strained to hear sounds upstairs—footfalls, doors creaking. I heard nothing. "I'm a detective, Miss Granger." I couldn't keep my mind off the picture of the woman.

"I see. Then will you tell me who is looking for Frank Plummer and what his interest in this person is?" Still business.

I needed a Lucky and some Overholt. This conversation was giving me a pain. "Look, Miss Granger," I said, "detectives are supposed to come around and ask questions and push people up against doors and tear their lapels and finally find out everything they want to know. Well, it's really not like that. I don't push people around. With my credit I couldn't get an apple ring down at the Spudnut. I paused to let the effect set in. "My client is someone who cares about Frank Plummer and pays me to keep his little secret, but he doesn't pay much. I don't want to hurt you, upset you, threaten you, or make you angry. It's just a question I have to ask, and you are the first person I asked on this bright Saturday morning. Give me a break?" I gave this sob speech once before at the door of a motel in El Dorado. That time I had a fistfight with the guy in 16B.

Carmen Granger laughed gently. I joined her. "All right," she said, giving me a smile. "I suppose I can help a poor fellow who can't even get an apple ring at the Spud-

nut." Still no creaking floorboards upstairs. The woman
outside the bay windows continued to dig and mulch. "I've
met Frank Plummer and gone out on dates with him. He's a
nice boy but a little wild for my somewhat refined taste."
She laughed again. "Actually, he really is too wild for me.
It doesn't amount to much beyond a family dispute and I
would rather not discuss that part of it with you."

"I see. When is the last time you saw him?"

"Yesterday evening. No, perhaps late yesterday afternoon." Last evening when I was dancing with Carl Plummer.

"Do you know where he is now?" I asked.

"I really couldn't say."

"Do you mean you couldn't say because you don't
know, or because you know, but you won't say? I get a
little snarled by these semantic pythons."

I saw a fire in the sapphire eyes. She glanced out the
window at the woman gardening, then back at me. "Mr.
Roberts, I have seen Frank Plummer. He has been my
escort in the past and it has caused some embarrassment to
me and my family. I spoke with him yesterday evening
about nothing consequential and he went away. I really
don't know where he is at this moment and am unwilling to
discuss my personal affairs with you further." Carmen
Granger at twenty could negotiate Jack Graybul out of his
trumpet.

"Do you know where I might start to look for him?" I
asked.

"His father owns a salvage yard, I believe."

"You mind telling me if Frank has any other friends who
might be of help in locating him?"

We sat there sipping gin and grapefruit juice. The Elgar
stopped. I really hate Elgar and was hoping that Ellington
or Basie would drop onto the invisible turntable. The day
outside was clouding over, turning gray and cooler. The
elms in the park danced in reflection on the parquet.

Carmen stuck her peachy lips against the frosted glass of

gin. "Please, Mr. Roberts. This is a simple matter between Frank and me. I don't know where he is. I don't know his friends and probably wouldn't sic you onto them if I did. I appreciate the fact that you have a job to do. But, you must appreciate my privacy and my need to conduct my affairs without interference."

I was thinking that now we had both delivered our prepared speeches and the score was tied.

I got up and put my glass on the silver tray. "Okay, Miss Granger, I'll lay off you for a while. But if I have to, I'll be back and you'll have to come off the Little Miss Muffet routine."

More fire in the sapphire.

"I'm sorry I forgot to wear lapels today," she said. "Now, please leave."

She walked me to the front door. I stood in the wind, turned, and said, "If you change your mind about this, for any reason, call me at my office. I'm on Lincoln. Roberts."

She said, "Good-bye," and closed the door. I stayed on the porch for a minute, then went around to the side of the house.

The woman kneeling in the rose garden watched me walk toward her. Then she stood, her blue sarong with pink water hyacinths billowing in the wind. She was taller than Carmen and older, a fuller figure, but with the same copper skin and deep sapphire eyes. She wore a white sweater. Her face was sculptured, not young and thin like Carmen's. I didn't think muscles and a good tan would mean a thing to her.

"Hello," I said, feeling the modulation in my voice that meant I was scared. Her neck was long and dreamy and she was high-waisted.

"Hello." Melodic.

I looked at the roses. "Hybrid polyantha?"

"Why, yes. Actually there is very little tea rose in this

one. It is beautiful, isn't it?" I shot a look at the upstairs windows of the house. No movement, no shadows.

"Yes," I said, "especially the yellow. What do you call them?"

"Texas Beautiful." She looked down at the rosebush. She had a pruning tool and trowel in her hands, gardening gloves. "Are you a rose lover?" She took off her straw gardener's hat. Her hair fell down her back, shining. I had expected it to be black, but it was auburn.

"Yes. My grandpa taught me a lot about roses. Water them every third day." I smiled. "Actually, my specialty runs to potatoes and squash. How is it you can nurse these by the heat of summer?"

She looked straight through me. I realized her eyes were deep green, not sapphire at all. Maybe they changed color in the light. I couldn't tell.

"I make a point of covering these special roses with cheesecloth during the hottest part of the day. I keep the cheesecloth damp. You mustn't let water touch the leaves. They will rust, and then one gets mites and mildew." She knew exactly how to hold her hands. I didn't. "Knowing how to prune in spring and fall is the secret to large flowers—and, of course, the water and nutrients."

"I guess it's a matter of care, then?"

"Of course."

I held out my hand. "I'm Mitch Roberts. I've just been visiting Carmen Granger in the house and saw the roses and thought I would find out their secret."

"My name is Carlotta. Carlotta Granger." We shook hands. She laughed. "Excuse the gloves," she said.

She went on. "The Texas Beautiful is my creation. If you look closely they are a very deep yellow and the petals are wide and strong. I registered the hybrid with the Rose Society."

I bent over and smelled the roses.

"No, there will be little or no fragrance. The more beautiful and cultivated the rose, the less its fragrance." She shook her hair free. "Don't worry," she said, "there are always lots of ramblers and climbers to make the air smell pretty in spring." She had seen a feigned worried look on my face. Our little joke. "Are you a friend of Carmen's?" I couldn't get over how she said the cultivated and beautiful roses didn't have a fragrance.

"No, Miss Granger," I said. "I'm a private detective looking for Frank Plummer."

"I see." That was what Carmen had said. "Did you have any luck?"

There was mystical intensity in Carlotta. She stood perfectly still in the wind, her sarong flapping. Concealed everything she was thinking. She was smart and beautiful and strong.

"Not exactly," I said.

"Then you didn't come over here to talk about my roses." She made it a statement and not a question.

"Yes and no." I answerred anyway. "I'm finished talking about roses, but they are still very beautiful."

"And now you want to talk about Frank Plummer?"

"Yes," I said, "and perhaps about your sister." It was getting too cool for seersucker. "Why don't we talk about this over lunch? If you don't have anything to say, at least you snatch a free lunch and get to be seen with me."

There was silence. A lion across the street yawned a roar. I felt Old Spice collecting in my white oxfords.

"Why not?" Thank God, she was smiling. "Let me clean up and change clothes. I'll pick you up in thirty minutes in front of the alligators. Wait for me there?" She disappeared around the back of the house. I heard a screen door shut.

I walked across the street and up Nims to the bird house. There were rows of cages out in the open. I leaned on the railing looking at the ring-necked pheasant and smoked a cigarette. There must have been five hundred thousand ring-necked pheasants in the stubble fields of western Kansas and this poor bastard ends up in the zoo. No fuck-ing, no flying, no eating corn. When I was a kid I used to come down to the pheasant cage and eat peanuts and try to get the pheasant to make his noise. It sounded like, "Ugh-OOOH, ugh-OOOH." I burned my throat making that noise until the pheasant ruffed his neck up and responded. It usually took an hour or so.

I thought about Carlotta Granger and about trying to get the pheasant to make his noise. A little girl in a blue sundress held a balloon next to my ear. She stared at me. It would have been too easy to put my Lucky out against the balloon and start her bawling. I walked over to where the alligators snoozed on wet sand and waited for Carlotta to pick me up in her pink Thunderbird. At least I hoped she belonged to the pink Thunderbird.

I was smoking and looking at the alligators sleep. Through the wire gondola over the alligator pit I saw Coal Barge and Buddy walking fast up the path. They looked mad. I knew another trip downtown meant I could collect my mail at the city dump. Behind me Carlotta pulled up in the little Thunderbird and gave a beep. Coal Barge and Buddy stopped and stood still. I walked to the Thunderbird and got in beside Carlotta.

"We're off," she said and smiled.

We drove down Murdock toward the bridge. I gave Coal Barge the finger and my best Sunday grin.

# FIVE

Behind us Coal Barge was a rictus and snap-brim hat steadily receding. Paddleboats in the river churned the muddy yellow water and a few canoeists glided their canoes under the bridge. It was all dragonflies and hoptoads. It was that time between summer and fall when the old man finally agrees to a picnic and loads the battered DeSoto with kids, some sandwiches, and a mushy watermelon. It was that time of afternoon at that time of year when the old man wishes he was home with a beer and a ball game. The clouds kicked themselves around enough to let some sunshine dapple the water and the red-brick street. Cottonwoods down by the riverbank flapped leaves in the wind like a field of wet silver sheets.

"Friends of yours?" Carlotta said, half smiling.

"Old bowling buddies. Guy on the left is Joe Joseph. On the right is his cousin, Pat Patterson. Parents blessed with lots of imagination."

"Funny," Carlotta said. "One of those gentlemen looks

very much like Detective Sergeant Davis. Perhaps just one of those silly coincidences."

"No way. Could not be. I met those guys years ago at the Civic Bowl at a marathon onion-ring-eating contest. No mistake, sure thing."

Carlotta kept her eyes on the road, glancing in the rearview mirror, but I could see she enjoyed the way things had started out, kind of a perverse sense of poking a finger in authority's eye.

Her hair curled up behind her in the open air, but strands of it came loose and wandered in the rush of wind. It was auburn when the sun glanced past it, shaded henna. She wore a shiny, ocean-green skirt that fit her like a steam bath, pale green high heels with a strap around her ankles. She showed enough long, nylon-wrapped leg to make a boy quit the church. Her laugh was nice and neat and very authentic. Still, there was tension in her, and she drove too fast, cutting in and out of traffic, beating lights to the punch. In Wichita, there is just no place to get to that fast.

Before long Carlotta was driving ten miles an hour over the speed limit. She changed lanes smoothly, always in control. Finally I asked her if she was hungry and she said, "I'm starved." I offered her a choice between Ralph Baum's Burger Bar on Kellogg Street or the Madrid Supper Club south of town out by the air base. By the time we got to the Madrid we called each other by our first names.

The Madrid isn't much more than a joint. It's a square box with a flat roof and flamenco dancers painted on the walls by some local sign painter. Three rows of tables clutter the floor, all set with candles and imitation roses in vases, a raised platform in one corner for the local cowboy bands on Friday nights, and a horseshoe bar in the middle of the room. We got a table and sat down. We were almost alone in the place.

"Is this what you call a roadhouse?" she asked as we picked up our menus.

"This is a true-blue roadhouse."

"It's kind of low."

"I know what you mean. Even the mice are hunch-backed."

She laughed and looked at the menu. "I'm having a good time. I haven't laughed like this in a long while. You don't know."

"Good," I said. "It suits you. I tell you. The steak sandwiches are great, or a big rib eye and enchiladas. Maybe some guacamole and fried cauliflower. The fries are greasy enough to lube a double trailer. What do you say?"

"It sounds so eclectic. What about steak and enchiladas and some guacamole?"

"Sold."

We ordered a pitcher of Hamm's, too. When it came I lit a Lucky, offered Carlotta one, and she took it. She asked me about myself and I told her about my mom who lived on a farm down in southeast Kansas and my Grandma Roberts who still rooted for the wrestlers on TV out of Pittsburgh and Joplin. I told Carlotta to dip some cauliflower in hot sauce and put vinegar on the fries. She was like a kid at Christmas. We finished the enchiladas over our second pitcher of cold brew.

"It's funny," I said, "but you don't particularly look or act like Bull Granger. Christ, you don't look like Bull Granger at all."

She stayed quiet for a while. Finally, she said, "He's not my father. He's my stepfather. He married my mother when I was in my early twenties. Carmen was quite a lot younger then."

"Your father?"

"My father died during the war. Carmen knew him only a little."

"I'm sorry," I said.

"It's all right. My father was a wonderful man. A doctor in the Navy. He was older and working on a hospital ship outside what was supposed to be the zone of action. Off

Okinawa in the last days. His ship was hit by kamikazes. He was lost with lots of other men."

"Your mother is the woman on the desk?"

"Yes."

"She is very beautiful."

"Yes, she was very beautiful. And gentle."

"Her daughters have the same quality."

Carlotta smiled, but without much heart. She looked at the bubbles in her glass of beer. I had been with her a couple of hours now and didn't want to get around to Frank Plummer and Bull Granger.

"Your mother is dead, too?" I asked. For fifty bucks a day I was turning gold to lead.

"Yes. She died five years ago in June." I was trying to think back to the headlines or the obituaries. Five years of muscatel was a lot of muscatel.

"I'm not sure I can see Bull Granger with your mother either. Perhaps I'm prying into things I shouldn't?" I tried to get it through my head that it was my fucking job to pry.

"No. It's all right. My mother met Bull in San Antonio. He was just Sergeant William Granger then. We lived there in the hills outside of town. A little ranch my father built. Bull was in training at the army base, doing something with the military police. Believe it or not, he was somewhat earnest and impressive. My mother was lonely and confused. She married him and brought us to Wichita. The rest is history, as they say."

I gave Carlotta another cigarette. She went on.

"It was hard for us. Bull turned out—well, perhaps you know."

"I think I do. The last time we chatted he called me a peckerwood and offered to make a necklace of my teeth."

"Yes. That's his style."

"I'm sorry, Carlotta," I said. "I like you a lot. I like being around you. But sometime soon we have to talk about Frank Plummer."

Carlotta said quietly, "Maybe we could drive a bit? Or just sit outside? I need some fresh air."

"I know just the place. I've got a mimosa tree, a rocker, and a refrigerator full of cold beer. What do you say?"

I paid the check. On the way out I saw a few airmen leaning on the horseshoe bar drinking. It would be six or seven hours before the serious fistfights started.

When we got outside, the sun slanted low through coral clouds bunched on the western horizon. Everything bathed in a silky glow. Carlotta drove the shady streets and told me about bringing up Carmen and about how Bull kept them both on a short string. The Hamm's was working on me, and as Carlotta drove through the crystal evening I fantasized my way from her knee on north. I directed Carlotta to my office and she parked in the gravel lot in front. We got out and went through the office to the backyard. I showed Carlotta the rocker and pulled up a paint bucket for myself. I got two cans of cold beer and sat down beside her.

We sat still, listening to the elms swishing and a couple of doves cooing. A red squirrel stood in the shaggy grass eating an acorn. We might have been alone on the face of the prairie. I liked that thought. Andy used to tell me that private detectives were better off in L.A. or Chicago because there was more action. After my divorce from Linda I decided I wanted quiet more than action. So far I had the quiet, all right.

We drank. The squirrel ate his acorn.

"How is it you can make it with the Bull? There doesn't seem any percentage in your trying to wait him out. I mean, it must be terribly difficult for you."

Something kept me from asking the questions that needed asking. Some of it was the way I saw the same lamentable look in Carlotta that I had seen in that picture on the desk. I sat on my paint bucket with my elbows on my knees and let smoke from my Lucky curl up in the breeze and fade. A train north of town, out by the grain elevators and refineries, blew an A minor seventh, the mournful sound gradually growing smaller and sadder.

"You know," she said, never taking her eyes off the motionless squirrel, "once I was standing with my mother across from police headquarters. I must have been in Wichita only about six months. Carmen was still a kid in school." She paused and gave me a little smile. "Anyway, my mother took me downtown that day to shop. We were going to meet Bull for lunch. There was something wrong with Mother then, some dreadful sadness. She kept to her room upstairs, hardly coming down. She cried. Wept, actually. We talked and she said she was homesick. But I knew a lot better. Bull was terrible. He bullied. He lied. He scared her with his violence and drinking. I heard them quarrel. Not quarrel really, just Bull and his terrible voice accusing Mother of things. Slut. Whore. Then, of course, he could be contrite, beg her forgiveness. When he was angry there was violence in the air that stopped everything. Time stopped.

"Well, anyway, I stood across the street from police headquarters with my mother after shopping. I remember she bought me some new white gloves. I wore this blue summer dress with big white polka dots and she wanted me to have some light white gloves for summer. I remember the day. Big puffy clouds and bright sunshine."

She stopped and took a drink of beer. Her voice was failing her a little bit. The squirrel sprinted up the mimosa, hopped a telephone wire, and disappeared in the bulky swirl of elms across the back fence.

She went on. "Bull wasn't Bull then. He was Detective Lieutenant Granger. Just like Davis outside today. A detective. We saw him pull up that day in an unmarked car followed by a squad car. In the backseat of the squad car one uniformed officer sat with a Negro woman. Another officer drove. Bull got out of the unmarked car and walked back to the squad car and opened the back door. The officers left the squad car and walked to the station-house door. Bull stayed. My mother and I just watched. We could hear everything. Bull leaned in the window, bent over with his forearms on the body of the door. 'Okay, bitch. Whore, out.' That's the way Bull talked to her. She moved to the door. Then he slapped her a little. Not too bad. Just a swipe with his hand across her face. She had this crazy red light in her eyes. I remember the hate in those eyes. The woman said something like 'Get off my case, you honky.' At that, Bull quickly kicked her leg in the open door and shut the door on her ankle. At first he shut it just tight enough to trap her foot. She stopped talking and leaned back with her elbows on the back seat. She was just waiting, breathing hard from her cursing, a look of concern creeping inside all that hate. Then Bull leaned on the door. The woman was terrified.

"Bull bent his knees then and worked on the door. The woman screamed. Oh, Mitch. You could hear her ankle break. A grisly pop. 'You gonna be fine now, bitch,' Bull said. I know he said that. The uniformed officers stayed by the door to headquarters, looking, not saying anything. Bull grabbed the woman by her bloody ankle. It was bent at a strange angle. He pulled her hard in one jerk out of the backseat and onto the pavement. She bounced on the edge of the car frame and then on the ground. She was lying there, crying.

"Bull made a sign to the officers at the door. They picked up the woman and dragged her into the station. When I looked at my mother, she had her fingers in her mouth and one hand on her forehead. Her face was terrible —paralyzed with hurt and fear. We left. I had to help her walk away."

"I'm sorry," I said. There wasn't a helluva lot to say.

I went into the storeroom and cracked two Pabsts and tore off a handful of Kleenex from the box on Gertie's desk. Gertie, I could tell, wouldn't mind at all. I came and sat down on my paint bucket. Carlotta held out her hand

for the tissues but I reached over and dabbed at the tears on
her cheeks myself.

"What if I get tipsy?" she asked.

"It's okay. I know this guy in Vice who can get you off a
public drunkenness charge." We looked at each other for a
moment and then laughed out loud. She was laughing and
crying at the same time. I thought she looked beautiful.

"What about you? How is it you can make it?"

"Oh, shit, Carlotta, I make it on muscatel, chess, and
baseball. Sometimes I get down my Hegel and go in for the
master-slave dynamic. Sometimes I don't think about it.
When I do, I don't see a helluva lot of formal order in the
world. Things sort of jumble together. Once in a while
something good falls out of the dumpster, but mostly it's
just other people's garbage and your own. Lots of ruined
crap. Discarded dolls, broken-backed books, glue bottles,
women's hose, that kind of stuff. Then there is the guy in
Hoboken who finds a thousand-dollar bill wadded up inside
a scumbag. Me, I look for Hanebrink or Matthews to dive
for a screamer down the third-base line and snag it over the
bag, come up throwing, and beat the guy at first by half a
step. I give a shit if the rest of the game nothing happens.
The catcher falls asleep. The vendors disappear. They give
away all the hot dogs. The beer goes flat. But there will be
one play Matthews made at third you can talk about in the
bar for the next six months."

"What about girls?" Carlotta said.

"I like 'em."

She said, "Haven't you married?"

"I got married once a long time ago," I said. "I was
drunk when I asked, I was drunk when I bought the ring,
and I was drunk when I said yes. I meant it at the time,
though."

"What happened?" She paused. "You don't seem that
way to me now. Here."

I ducked the question. "How old was your father when
he went in?"

She frowned. "He was fifty-three. He was fifty-seven when he died. He was in the Reserves for a long time. He wanted to go in even though we all told him he could stay in San Antonio and work at the hospitals there and do just as much good. He told us that doctors never got killed in wars. He said that a lot. In all his letters. Doctors don't get killed in wars. Don't worry. In his last letter, it was in the summer, he said that we were beating them badly now. The war wasn't over yet because the fat lady hadn't sung yet. He'd be home when he could hear the fat lady singing. He could hear her warming up in the wings. Then he died."

She looked down. "I'm sorry. Please. Why did you want to know?"

"I was in the same war. Different part. I was just a kid when I went in. Twenty-two. I was gonna be a flier. Sit around pubs and drink whiskey and smoke English cigarettes. Wear a black leather jacket with a skull on the back. Maybe a blue silk scarf. I got to England and found out every kid who joined the Army applied for the Air Corps. Five thousand airplanes and fifty thousand hotshots looking for jobs flying them, all sitting around in their dreams in a black jacket drinking whiskey. I went into the Engineers because that's what they told me I volunteered to do. One day I woke up and I was strapping dynamite to tank traps on a French beach, machine-gun bullets whizzing around, and mortars exploding on the beach. It was before dawn and the water was cold as hell and there were guys screaming and dying everywhere. I was scared. But, then I made it through and things got better. When we got across the Rhine, all the guys started talking about home like it was a real place. No one dies anymore, we all go home.

"Then one day my four buddies and I found this old house on the outskirts of a little Alsatian town, kind of a villa with a little pond, a couple of sheds for tools and cheese and meat, a big mountain house with a veranda. We got into the wine cellar and there must have been a hundred bottles of champagne, vermouth, and old French brandy.

We found meerschaums with carved figures on the bowls. Tobacco that smelled like apples. This one scrawny goose wandering around the pond we caught and stuck him on a spit over a fire we built. It was April and the pear trees were in bloom and the bees were buzzing their heads off. In this one closet I found a trunk full of hats. There were four or five opera hats, you know, shiny black top hats that pop up when you hit the bottom. Hey! Top hats. Yeah! So my buddy Joe Smith gets the other guys together and they put on these top hats and pass brandy and tobacco. Joe and I, we had been on the beach together and we looked for land mines all the way from Calais to the Rhine. I had this old box camera with me that I took pictures with. Bridges we built. Bridges we blew up. The Eiffel Tower. Bullet holes in the art museum. Anyway, I got the guys bunched together and snapped their picture. When I snapped I heard a sharp crack behind me. I put the camera down. There was an echo in the valley. It was the report of a bullet. When I looked around, I saw the guys bunched around Joe. His legs twitched once. One hand was in a fist. I walked over and looked at him. There was a pure blue bullet hole in his forehead. As they say, he never knew what hit him. I've still got the goddamn picture. Four guys in tops smoking pipes. A brandy bottle at one guy's lips. Joe had a big smile. The guy next to him had his arm draped in a Vee over Joe's shoulder. I look at that picture and know that the bullet is in that picture, stopped forever. The goddamn bullet is in the picture."

I looked at Carlotta. She was serene in the dusk. A few early stars twinkled overhead. To the east between the elms I could see a bank of lights glowing. At the stadium the guys in left field would be warming up, catching flies over their shoulders and chewing tobacco, not giving a thought to invisible bullets in tangible photographs, not to speak of crushed ankles and Bull Granger.

"Why don't you just make a break for it?" I asked. "Get out of this crummy little town and leave old Bull behind?"

"Yes, why not?" Her face got hard and her eyes narrowed. "You see, old Bull took my mother for every penny she had. Sold the ranch and put the money in the house in Riverside and in College Hill where he lives now. Dear old Bull lets us live in the Riverside house, but he owns it. Owns everything now. Do you think I should go to work down at Woolworth's? My stepfather threatens us both with such things. And worse."

"How about some legal action?"

"It won't work. I've checked."

She put her face close to me.

"I hate him so terribly, so desperately. For what he did to my mother. For how he changed my life. And for Carmen."

"What does Carmen feel?"

"She feels the same." She straightened up and shook her auburn hair. There were tears in her eyes. I couldn't tell if she was laughing or crying.

I got up and went to the storeroom to get more Kleenex. When I got back I reached over and dabbed the corners of her eyes. I was looking at Carlotta and then I kissed her and she kissed back. She tasted like beer and salt. I moved back a bit to look her over, but when I did she grabbed me and held on and kissed me some more. Then we came out of the clinch, the bell rang, and we went to the corners to get worked on by cut men and managers.

"Can I trust you, Mitch?" Carlotta whispered.

"Why not? Now that we've gone all the way."

Carlotta smiled at my little joke. "Frankie Plummer is crazy. He's got something on the Bull, something that lets Frankie get away with things no one else could. He comes and goes at the Riverside house. He terrifies Carmen and the Bull won't stop it. Usually, the Bull reserves that honor for himself. I think Frankie is blackmailing the Bull."

Carlotta stared at me with frightened eyes. She was wringing her hands.

"You don't have any idea what it's all about?" I asked.

"No, but the Bull is capable of anything."

Carlotta brushed the hair away from the corner of her mouth and sighed again deeply.

"Will you try and get Frankie away from us? Talk to the Bull? I can take it myself, but I can't stand to see Carmen dragged into this terrible mess. She's such a kid."

"I already have a client, you know."

"Can't you do it anyway?"

"Well, I guess there is nothing to the International Code of Ethics for private detectives to prevent me doing a favor for a friend. I'll check around. See what there is."

Carlotta smiled and put her hands on my shoulders. She put her cheek on mine.

"God, thank you," she said.

We left the office and Carlotta drove slowly back to Riverside and the park. We crossed the Murdock Bridge. There were just a few canoes left in the water. The old boathouse dock creaked as waves lapped its side. It wasn't dark yet, but the street lamps in the park cast hesitant halos in the dusk. We stopped beside my Ford and Carlotta leaned over and kissed me hard. I kissed back. Somehow, I was doing it against my better judgment. I got out and stood in the street watching Carlotta turn the T-bird and disappear behind the bears, then appear between the ostriches, and drive into the driveway of the old house on Nims.

I got in my car and dug the binoculars from under the front seat. I put them on Carlotta. She drove up to the carriage house, got out, opened the doors to the shed, lit a cigarette, and went up the porch steps to the front door. Carmen opened the door, they embraced, and both were swallowed by the shadows in the front room.

There was no blue Pontiac. Carlotta parked in the shed like there wouldn't be a blue Pontiac in the near future.

I started the Fairlane and drove around the neighborhood

for about five minutes looking for dusty blue Plymouths. I didn't find any. I drove out of Riverside wondering where all the blue cars filled with blackmailers and cops had gone. Just yesterday they were a big deal.

And then there were Carlotta's lies to think about.

# SIX

It was growing dark as I drove out of the wooded park and across the Nims Street Bridge. Light from the copper lamps on the bridge danced in the river water, mingled with the reflection of lighted buildings from downtown. My head buzzed from the two pitchers of beer and several salty, hard kisses. I let the smoke from my Lucky drift out of my mouth and rush past my ear. There was a softness in the air, a feel of the heat breaking down; I could sense summer losing its legs in the middle rounds and starting to sag against the ropes. The cicadas no longer gave out a raucous uproar and the squirrels were intent and purposeful, not dallying and chattering anymore. I reminded myself to check the fuzz on caterpillars to see if winter was going to be a bitch or not.

I drove down a nearly deserted Central Street, past the closed stores, avoiding the crowds of teenagers who flock to the main drag to drive their new Chevys and Fords, looking for some kind of excitement from a town that goes

61

to sleep at ten. What I needed was a piss and some time to think.

Carlotta expected me to believe that Carmen was terri-fied of Frankie Plummer and walked around the big house in Riverside like a zombie in distress, or maybe like an unraveling mummy. But I had taken a pretty good look at Carmen and she was fresh and cool as a gherkin on ice. I tried to remember a ruffle in her come-on, some sort of crack in that lacy and dignified demeanor, but couldn't. She seemed in control. It was my guess that unless she was a pretty good actress there wasn't anything on her mind that involved being held hostage against her will by some ducktailed punk like Frankie Plummer.

I was in and around the house for about an hour and there was no sign of Frankie. No cigarette butts, girlie magazines, creaking floorboards. No smell of lilac water. If Frankie Plummer was in that house it looked to me like he was the one being held hostage. If he was upstairs in that strange old house, then he was holding his hill-boy breath.

For some reason, I had let it pass with Carlotta that I had seen Carmen driving Frankie's big blue Pontiac at midnight on Friday night. The way Carmen roared over the Nims Bridge and into the carriage house, it was clear she was coming and going in a hurry. It didn't make sense that she was being held against her will and terrorized when she had taken the kid's wheels and scooted around town like a pasha. Somebody was bullshitting me. When I started making a list of the people talking crap, it turned out that almost everybody I spent any time with in the last two days was spreading it around for the flies. Carl Plummer. Andy Lanham. Carmen and Carlotta. Even the Bull just slapped me around a little when he and the boys could have served my bones for dinner to the guys doing sixty days on the p-farm.

This thing was getting to be the hall of screwy mirrors at the State Fair. Carl Plummer hires me to find his kid and then tells me where to go to put a finger on him. So Plummer the Elder probably wants me just to flush the kid out of his hiding place and keep track of his movements. Why? The cops are interested in the same information, so Coal Barge and Buddy hang around like buzzards on a rail. They try to run me off before I steal a bite of the skunk they have spotted in the road.

The tea leaves said that Bull Granger and Carl Plummer had the same interest in Frankie, but worked the opposite sides of the street. Carl hires me to hang around and peep; Bull runs me off.

I flipped on the Philco and got Nat King Cole singing "Tangerine." The porch sitters were out and I could see them rocking on the swing and smoking. When Nat finished with "Tangerine," Jimmy Fiddler came on with some strident nonsense about Linda Darnell and Cornel Wilde. I'd rather hear the farm report.

What got me was the fact that I was stooging for Carlotta. She wanted free of Bull and she wanted revenge. She was deeply damaged by the knockout Bull gave her mother, but how she expected to get free—and get her money and her revenge—was still obscure. But if Carlotta and Carmen had on their boxing gloves, I had no way of knowing what their best punch could be. In that case it's always best to watch the guy's navel. Come to think of it, I wouldn't mind watching Carlotta's navel for a while anyway. Carl Plummer was giving me fifty a day and Carlotta was sticking hard kisses on my mouth and old Mitch just shucked corn down at the crib. It was time to start tying my own shoes and catching the school bus on my own. It was time to get some answers and play the game for keeps.

I got across town to the Uptown Recreation about seven o'clock and pulled up in the bus stop. The door to the Wreck was open and from inside came the jukebox sound of Johnnie Ray and the muffled blather common to joints all over the country. Cheap conversation and watered beer.

I flipped off the ignition and sniffed at the stale odor of

beer and nuts flooding from the open door. It was a hell of a way to make a living, prowling grimy bars, rubbing elbows with thugs and grifters. I should have been upside down at the third level of Carlsbad Caverns.

The answer I needed most was why the cops weren't interested in Frankie Plummer anymore. On Friday he's the crown jewels; on Saturday he's a dandelion in a wheat field. Whatever made Frankie interesting to the cops on Friday was gone.

The inside of the Wreck was deep in neon and sepia. Johnnie Ray gave way to the Platters. There were a couple of guys shooting snooker on the first table by the bar. A sign on the wall said NO GAMBLING. There was a ten-spot by the corner pocket and the two guys walked around the table silently, shooting snooker for the ten-spot. At the end of the bar Kenny Shoemaker sat sucking on a draft and smoking a Camel.

"Mitch!" he boomed.

"Hi, Shoe, how are you?" Without waiting for an answer I said, "Shoe, you know where Tony might be?"

"Back room," he said. "Hey, by the way, did I tell you what happened to me the other night out at the Moose Club. The fucking dime slots. I got this girl shacked down in Haysville and we were out at the Moose playing the fucking dime slots."

I interrupted. "I'll be back, Shoe. Keep it in your pants for a while. I gotta talk to Tony right now."

"Okay, Mitch," Shoe said.

I skirted the snooker tables and went into the back room. Tony was lifting a case of Budweiser bottles. He saw me and smiled.

"Be right with you, Mitch," he said. He got his case stacked up on the top of a pile of empties and turned around.

"I figgered I'd be seeing you."

"Well, here I am. You know why I'm here."

Tony said, "Let's go out in the alley."

We went through the back door and into a dark alley that separated the snooker hall from the Uptown movie theatre. The current show was *Wichita* with Joel McCrea. The goddamn world premiere. Tony cracked a Pabst and held it out to me.

"Tony," I said, "you and me, we've known each other for a long time, right?"

Tony fidgeted and nodded yes.

"I figure if it wasn't for me that fat lady would have made your liver a little drafty. I figure a couple of times I bail your dumb kid out of his speeding rap because I go talk to Andy at headquarters. Half a dozen times the cops out of Vice come down here and ask you why you are sitting around blowing reefer and drinking beer with the customers at three in the morning when closing time is midnight and reefer is against the law. The goddamn pinball machines pay off. I call Andy, he talks to a couple of the boys, and you are still sitting pretty instead of doing ten up in Lansing. Your old lady has a husband, your kids still got a father."

I looked at Tony. "How'm I doing so far?" I asked.

"I can't wait for the fucking punch line," Tony said.

"So, anyway, I been knocking around the gutters of this village for quite a few years. Nothing big, mind you. Then all of a sudden I hear about this guy Frankie Plummer. The cops don't know nothing about him. Sure. I don't know nothing about him. Even the kid's old man don't know nothing about him. So, old Mitch here, he's pissing in the wind. Getting it on his trousers. He comes to his old buddy Tony for some information. He figures Tony is good for the truth because Tony is Tony. You tell me this morning you don't know shit about Frankie Plummer. I say you and everybody else I talk to about this fucker are liars and scumbags."

I hit the Pabst. "That's the punch line, Tony," I said.

"It ain't like that, Mitch. Really it ain't."

"Let me explain something," I said. "Make it clear so even a dumb fuck like Tony Garcia can understand it."

Tony weighed in at two-thirty-five and I was hoping he wouldn't get mad. If he did, I would have to go for the blackjack in a big hurry.

I went on. "Bull Granger wants this Frankie Plummer for some reason I don't know why. Frankie's old man, this junkyard hill man, wants his kid, but not bad enough to go right on in and get him out of his hole, wherever that is. I get a feeling even the goddamn newsboy down on Douglas and Main knows what the fuck is going on. Not me, Tony. I don't know shit. You sit there and tell me you don't know either, you're a goddamn liar."

Tony was quiet. I washed my anger down with a gulp of suds. "Tony, you owe me a goddamn honest fucking answer."

The last of sunset smoldered on the horizon.

"Mitch, I know you're shitting me a little bit. But you make me feel bad too." Tony looked at the ground and dug a pack of Pall Malls out of the back of his jeans.

"Look, I know we gone down some miles with each other. You done some nice things for my kid. We had some good times," he said.

I waited. There was something on Tony's mind and I was gong to hold on and let it come out in its own sweet time.

"You got a punch line for this?" I asked.

"I got a punch line, but you ain't gonna like it."

"Try me."

"What if," Tony said, "there's some kind of shit going down around here that's bigger than we can handle. Bigger than we want to handle. The kind of shit, you can get in but you can't get out. I ain't talking about sitting around blowing reefer, no fucking speeding ticket for the kid. No shitting around and drinking a few beers and being buddies."

Tony stopped talking while some guy in a dusty Stude-

baker pulled into the alley and turned around. From the
theatre there was a sound of a gunfight in the cow-town
streets of Wichita, then a crescendo of music that meant
the bad guy was dead and Joel McCrea was getting a big
hug from Vera Miles.

"Hey, man, you know there's only one thing worse than
anything else, right?" Tony said.

"You mean like waking up on Sunday with no private
stash of muscatel and finding Kenny is out of town?"

"No, man," Tony said. "I mean being dead. Fucking
dead. No more muscatel, no more nooky, no nothing."

"What're you saying, Tony?"

"I'm saying, man, if we mess around in this shit we
gonna wind up in half a tuxedo down at Maple Grove.
Dancing with the fucking worms. I can't deal with it, man.
I cannot fucking deal with it."

"I can," I said. "I'm the one who has to deal with it.
Right?"

"No, man, that ain't right. I tell you. This shit you are
into. I think you get in far enough some guy is gonna come
around and he's gonna have some pals behind him. They're
gonna get you in a corner somewhere and kick the shit out
of you. Then one of these guys is gonna ask who you been
talking to. Where you get your information. You know? It
didn't just fall out of the sky like pigeon shit. Then one guy
pulls out an acetylene torch. They ask you again, where
you get the information. These guys hold you down and
put that fucking torch to your hand and you tell them: Tony
Garcia, he told me everything. It was Tony Garcia. And
hey, man, I would do the same fucking thing. So then these
guys come looking for me. You dig?"

It wasn't Aristotle or Maimonides, but it was pretty
tight.

"Hey, let's start out slow," I said. "Let's take one thing
at a time. You come to a place you can't tell me then we
talk it over and see if we can figure a way around your
problem. Okay? Here we go."

Tony stomped his Pall Mall out with the heel of his work boot. He rubbed his eyes wearily.

"Bull Granger had a wife. Five, six years ago. Maybe more. She died. You know her?"

"Man," Tony said, "you shoulda let that fat lady do me in. Yeah. Where you been? Old lady Granger took a dive, couple of twists, maybe a gainer. But, you know, she missed the pool."

"How? When?"

"Late Forties. Dove out of the sixth floor of police headquarters. Shit, that ain't far enough to really kill you right off. Not her anyway. Lived for a while."

"Suicide?"

"Well," Tony said, "if I was married to the Bull I'd give it up too. Except I'd take the fucker with me when I went. Maybe it's possible that Bull drove her out the window. Nobody said much and the coroner came back real quick. How'm I doing?"

"Great," I said. "Now, what about Frankie Plummer?"

"Here is where we got a problem," Tony said. "You got the answer like you said?"

"All right. You say some big guy is gonna put the flame on my mitts. Suppose I give them somebody else. Maybe I got somebody else's name to scream out and scream it loud enough they're gonna let up a little."

"I don't know," Tony said.

"Say we give them the Toddler."

"Oh, man, who's gonna believe the Toddler knows shit?"

The Toddler was a small-timer who lived in the basement of one of the old pastel-colored apartment houses on Oakland Street just behind the Uptown Recreation. Oakland wound downhill for about two blocks. The street was overrun with drifters, runaway kids, and beatniks.

"Hey, Tony, what do they know? The Toddler runs a little reefer, does some hot cars. Right? Maybe he heard it from somebody else."

"I don't know," Tony said.

I waited. I didn't say anything.

The Shoe stuck his head out the back door.

"Hey, you guys. What is this shit?" he said. "I'm a customer and I'm taking snooker money, drawing beers, and making change. You guys getting married out here in the alley or something?"

Tony stepped toward the door. I put my hand on his chest and pushed him back a little.

"Hey, Shoe," Tony said, "take care of the bar for me for a little while, willya?"

"Uh, yeah, sure, I guess so," Shoe said. He ducked back inside.

"Hey, look," Tony said. "I tell you what I know and we're even, right?"

"We'll see. We're friends no matter what. You tell me the truth, that's all. That's my main fucking interest."

Tony leaned back.

"It's like this," he said. "Maybe a little heroin gets into this town. Not much but a little. There ain't much here to stay, but maybe a lot moves through. You follow, right?"

"So far, Tony, I can follow this real good."

"Yeah, well," he continued. "You know there's a man here in town who has the corner on that kind of shit. Well, this man has the shit trucked to the big boys in Chicago and Kansas City, but he keeps a little for his trouble and he makes some pocket change. You know, he keeps himself in Packards and blondes."

"Like Johnny Rossiter," I said.

"Like maybe," Tony said.

"Well, this man here he has his helpers and his assistants. Sometimes he needs a little executive cover just to oil the bearings and keep things running smooth."

"Will you cut the crap," I said. "Granger provides the executive cover."

"Hey, man," Tony said, "this is hard for me. Okay, so let's say there's an old junkyard hill man who is one of the assistants. He has this business connection with the main man. So the junkyard man sees to it that the shipment gets into town and gets to the main man. The junkyard man ain't nothing but a messenger, a middleman, but he is handling some very hot shit for the main man. That makes this main man very interested in the junkyard man because he pays the junkyard man to see that the shit arrives and gets to the main man so the main man can get it to Chicago. Say something goes wrong. The shit comes to town, the junkyard man takes delivery, and something goes wrong. Then the junkyard man has lots of trouble. But, hell, nothing ever goes wrong. The shit comes into town, the junkyard man takes the shit to the main man who takes a cut and sends it along to the boys in Chicago and Kansas City. A nice working arrangement for everybody, right?"

"I follow," I said, "but I could use some subtitles."

"All right. So the junkyard man has this kid. This kid is definitely bad. Wild. One day, say, the kid takes the shipment that the main man is supposed to get and holds everybody up for some bread. Nobody knows where the shit is except for the kid. Hell, maybe they don't know where the kid is. The kid wants to take his old man out of the play, take over the business sorta. You can see how this makes the junkyard man feel. Of course, the main man is most upset."

"So," I said, "why don't the junkyard man and the main man move in on the kid and put a blue flame to his fingers?"

"Yeah, well, that's a neat one, that one is. You know, Mitch, I don't the fuck know the answer. I just don't."

"One thing more, Tony," I said. "You know how sometimes Vice will come around and find some reefer in the corner pocket of the third snooker table and somebody gives the Vice guys twenty and it will just not turn into a major problem?"

"Yeah."

"So, like I said before. Granger provides cover for the main man? For Rossiter?"

"Listen, I don't know. How do you figger Granger owns a couple of houses and drives a Packard? I don't know."

Tony took a deep breath. "Hey, man," he said, "what do you think? You think that shit comes into this town and out to Kansas City and Bull Granger doesn't get a cut for keeping the guys off the main man's ass? How the fuck do I run the nickel machine, play slots out at the fucking Moose? Fuck, yes, man. Bull Granger and a couple of his stooges protect the main man. That's how it works, it always has worked, and always will."

"Okay, Tony," I said. "Thanks."

Tony walked around me and got half inside the back door. He stopped and turned.

"Stay out, Mitch. I don't know any of these guys. You know I don't mess with heroin and I don't mess with the main man and I don't mess with Plummer. Hell, I don't even know these guys. But some heavy shit is coming down now that the kid has jumped with a delivery. Hell, I don't even know where the kid could go to hide. But look, there is a lot of dough riding on this one and these guys get very upset and play rough."

Tony went inside. I could only see the red glow of his Pall Mall. He said, "You know I don't think they would put the flame to you anyway, Mitch. I think they might just kill your ass right off, you know?"

"Then the Toddler's got no problems. Right, Tony?"

He laughed. "Yeah. The Toddler's got no problems. See ya, Mitch. Be careful."

Then Tony was inside. I walked out of the alley and around to Hillside.

I drove slow uphill on Douglas and into College Hill toward Bull Granger's house. Three-story houses, big lawns, elm trees, and fancy cars. If you got to be rich you got to be here.

So Frankie Plummer copped a shipment of heroin from

Carl and Johnny Rossiter and split. He was trying to muscle in on the heroin-delivery business his old man ran for Rossiter. And Tony couldn't figure out where Frankie was hiding. Carmen and Carlotta and Frankie—what a happy family. Nothing made sense unless Carlotta fit in somewhere. She had to.

I had it figured that Carmen meets Frankie and they hatch a plot together. Frankie wants the heroin and the heroin-delivery business, and Carmen wants money and revenge on the Bull. As a team they are dynamite. They hide the heroin and hold the Bull up. The main man is steamed. He wants his heroin and the Bull's daughter knows where it is. But the main man can't squeeze Bull's daughter, and the Bull can't squeeze anybody because if he squeezes his own step-daughter the whole world finds out about it and Bull is out of business. The main man can't move on anybody because the Bull is in a spot. So Carmen and Carlotta and Frankie are standing off Carl and Rossiter and the Bull. Altogether, it is a very delicate situation.

One thing I couldn't figure exactly. Carlotta wanted me to roust the Bull and she lied about her involvement with Frankie. Maybe she just wanted me to horn in and make the Bull even more nervous. Maybe make him come across with some dough a little faster. But the heroin was missing and Carmen and Carlotta and Frankie knew where it was. Things didn't fit any other way.

I remembered I hadn't eaten anything since that rib eye and guacamole. I decided to cruise Bull's house in College Hill and then head home for a shower, some grub, and maybe the last four innings of the Braves game.

I thought about kissing Carlotta. Then two and two started making four and I knew how Mitch was going to cut himself in on this deal.

# SEVEN

College Hill doesn't have a college, and only if you were a myopic spider from somewhere around Lubbock would you think it was a hill. There is just an oblong clay mound that rises slightly above the plains where the Arkansas River runs through plum thickets and where the deer and the antelope used to play before the white man shot them all to death. Just after the deer and the antelope disappeared, the city fathers convened and decided the mound would be a good place for the local emporium for higher education, so they planted elms and cottonwoods and redbuds and platted streets with names like Vassar and Yale. It turns out the center for higher education became a modestly unimportant private university on the other side of town. The mound turned out to be College Hill, where modestly important bankers, businessmen, and doctors pursue modestly banal lives.

Driving up a tree-lined Douglas Avenue from Hillside and into the heart of College Hill you can see the elms and cottonwoods wax brawnier, the lawns grow bluer and more expansive, the cars longer and more glittery. The driveways in this part of town on Sunday morning look like a Lincoln-Mercury showroom where guys in pink bow ties and buckteeth wait with a handshake and a finger puzzle for the kiddies. On the hill's leeward slope the lawyers and college teachers hang on with their wives and house payments and one and a half bathrooms. On the flats, near the Catholic elementary school, a few Boeing engineers, high school counselors, and dentists are keelhauled in the invidious social wake.

College Hill was a beehive for the white middle class, the class that elected Eisenhower over Stevenson. If you got all the way up to Belmont Street on College Hill, you stopped being a worker and became a drone. Bull had made it to Belmont.

I cruised with the top down, trying to clear my head. I hadn't taken a piss back at the Uptown Wreck and my back teeth needed life jackets.

The entrance to Belmont off Douglas is embraced on either side of the street by two imposing stone pillars engraved with the name BELMONT. A grill fretwork arch connects the two pillars. A medieval copper lamp swings from the fretwork and the dancing light from its single bulb casts eerie shadows.

Bull Granger lived in the middle of the block on the east side of the street. I had decided earlier today that the best policy was to know the enemy on his own ground before making any definite moves. So I decided to get to know Bull Granger and Carl Plummer before cutting myself in on this heroin deal. It was an instinct for caution I picked up one starry night in a foxhole near Cherbourg.

Bull Granger lived in a Tudor mansion wrapped in a cocoon of lilacs, redbuds, and elms. A circular front porch was surrounded by a low stone wall, where ivy grew in profusion. In back was a double garage built like the house and separated from it by fifteen feet. Stairs wound up to the second floor of the garage, some sort of quarters for a servant if there was such a thing, or maybe a half-wit demented brother nobody wants to see.

I drove past Bull's house, around the corner, and parked in deep shadow under a cedar.

I took off my seersucker coat and tie and threw them in the backseat. Then I slid the blackjack under the front seat and strapped on an old pair of sneakers in place of my oxfords. I strolled up First Street in the dark and turned down Belmont toward Bull's, whistling "Jimmy Crack Corn" and trying to look for all the world like a weary real-estate entrepreneur on his evening perambulation.

Four conspiratorial tykes huddled at the base of an elm tree and put their eyes on me.

"Hello, men," I said. They stood there like a herd of zebra sniffing a lion in the bush. "Playing a little football, huh? Getting to be that time of year, I guess."

There were four boys, two of them either brothers or built from the same Erector set. They had the usual complement of towheads, cowlicks, missing teeth, scrapes, torn jeans knees, and ripped elbow patches. They wore Wichita Braves hats.

"Hello, mister," the tallest said. He was blond and had a voice like Froggy on Andy Devine's show.

I looked at Bull's Tudor mansion. There were no lights in any of the windows, but a gaslight burned in the front yard and there was a single bulb glowing over the garage doors. No cars in the driveway, and from what I could see no cars in the garage either. From the rest of the houses on the block a deadly blue glow reflected on the lawns. The people were inside somewhere numbing their brains on Two for the Money and George Gobel.

"You boys live around here?" I asked.

"Sure, right here," Froggy said.

"You gents know old Mr. Granger?"

"We might. Huh, fellas?" Froggy said. He was estab-

lished as the spokesman for the guys. The two shrimpy
redheaded brothers scurried in an effort to hide behind each
other and the elm tree that served as a goalpost. The fourth
kid was a fatty. He picked his nose and pretended to exam-
ine the results. The three of them nodded in unison when
Froggy looked their way.

"Listen, you guys, I'm a detective on a case." Froggy
looked at Fatty and they all giggled.

"Sure," Froggy drawled. "You can't fool us."

"Hey, this is no kidding. I'm a detective on a case and
I'm trying to get some information on Mr. Granger. You
kids could be of help on the case. You know, like the
Hardy boys. It's a big mystery and I can't trust just anyone.
Anyone I trust I gotta know is square and won't rat on me
or tell me lies. That's the way it is in the detective business
where you're into a big mystery."

"What do you want?" Froggy asked. The two tadpoles
behind the elm-tree goalpost edged their way out when
they heard the Hardy boys mentioned.

"You guys be my helpers and I'll let you in on the mystery and there will be a little cash in it for you. Only you
gotta promise not to tell anybody, especially your folks or
Mr. Granger. It's part of the deal."

"Yeah, so what else?" Froggy.

I paused for the dramatic effect. "You guys like Mr.
Granger?" I asked in my best conspiratorial tone.

Froggy shrugged and looked at the ground. The tadpoles
wriggled out and stood behind Froggy and Fatty like
shadows.

"Nah," Fatty said. "He's kind of a squirrel."

"Yeah, a real drip," said Froggy. So I had established
that Bull was a squirrel and a drip. This was real progress.

"What seems to be the problem?" I asked.

"My dad says he doesn't belong here," Fatty whined.

"He's just a mean tub," said Froggy. Between the social
explanation from Fatty and the metaethical one from
Froggy, I preferred the latter.

"See," I said, "I don't like Mr. Granger either. I want you guys to keep watch of the house tonight. Stay up as late as you can and when I come back around here tomorrow tell me what time Mr. Granger comes in and if he sees anyone. It might be as late as eleven or twelve o'clock."

"We stayed up that late before," Froggy said eagerly.

I dug into my wallet and got out four ones.

"Here's four dollars for you guys. When I come back, let me know when Mr. Granger comes in tonight, and keep an eye on him tomorrow. Kind of see who he's with and where he goes and when he comes home. There's another dollar in it for each of you tomorrow. That is, if you can keep a secret and do a good job. I'll come back here around five o'clock before supper. You guys be around?"

"Sure, mister," Froggy croaked. The gang checked their new dollar bills.

"I'll be here," Fatty said. The tadpoles were speechless.

"I'll see ya then."

I walked down the block and around onto Douglas where an alley split the block, turned up the alley back toward Bull's house, and stood behind the trash cans and rose trellises. The mansion looked about the same, dark and forlorn. But there wasn't any vicious mastiff with razor teeth and a spike collar.

By the time I drove home, my molars were being used as life vests on the SS *Hamm*'s. I made my way slowly around the side of the house. It was when I got to the porch that I saw the two-tone tan and brown DeSoto parked in front, a ghostly outline in the haze of left-field lights at Lawrence Stadium. A youthful smirk that looked like it might belong to Gomez leaked from the passenger window. The shadow behind the wheel probably belonged to someone who would back Gomez if it came down to brass tacks. I shuffled over, feeling rather ridiculous in seersucker pants and sneakers.

"Señor Gomez. What a pleasant surprise. And you come with your friend Cantinflas, no doubt."

Gomez called me a name, a series of them actually, in Spanish. My guess was that mother, my dog, and a dozen sailors from the *Arizona* could all take offense.

Finally, he added, "I have been sent here by Mr. Plummer."

"Which Mr. Plummer?" I asked. "I mean a guy like you Frankie Plummer probably pushes around easy."

"Hey, fuck you, shit! He don't push nobody around now."

Gomez stopped short. The shadow spoke in Spanish and there was a rondo and then a volley that echoed from here to El Paso. I figured I might force Gomez into a quick mistake and he had let one slip. Get a punk hot like that and his mouth runs by itself. They were trying to put the slip straight. Too bad Gomez didn't speak German. *That* I could understand.

"It's hard to tell about Frankie, right? I mean, I been looking for the handsome devil all day and he just won't turn up. You seen him, Gomez?"

Gomez stuck his greasy overalled arm over the door frame and growled, "The boss don't need you anymore. He says for you to get off the case."

"Did Frankie climb back into his plush trailer out behind the cottonwoods? You know, Gomez. The tin can that sits in the sun and doesn't have any running water?"

"All I know is Mr. Plummer he says he knows where Frankie got to and he don't need you no more. You get the fuck off and stay off. He don't like you anyway. I don't either." I remembered my blackjack under the front seat and wondered if I could handle two kids and two knives and a set of tire chains. It would have been easier if I didn't need a piss quite so badly.

"When did Frankie come home?" I asked.

"Today," Gomez said. There was another Spanish cadenza. "I mean Mr. Plummer told me today he didn't need

you anymore. I don't know where Frankie is. I ain't seen
him." Gomez was mad and making another mistake. He
had told me why Plummer wanted me off the case and that
he had seen Frankie. Turn on the boy's temper and his
smarts drained out of his asshole.

"What time does Carl Plummer want me to come and
report to him the results of this investigation?" The
longer I kept this jackrabbit on the spit, the more mis-
takes he was bound to make. It was a working hypoth-
esis, anyway.

"You don't come out to the salvage lot." Gomez was
tough again. He blew his nose by pressing a thumb against
one nostril and letting go with the other. His droppings
landed by my sneakers. I was too tired to draw a line and
dare him to step over.

"Doesn't he want to know what I found out about the
game being run by Carlotta? And the stuff?" When this got
back to Carl it would make the same kind of hit Gypsy
Rose Lee made in Chicago.

"What are you talking about, man?"

"What are you Gomez, some kind of a numbnuts or
something?"

"You better watch out."

"That's what I *have* been doing. Watching out."

"Say," Gomez sneered, "they gonna be eating that
skinny white dick of yours for sausage down at the Ma-
sonic Home."

"So long, punk," I said softly. "You been very helpful."

"I will see you again," Gomez replied. The DeSoto
jerked into gear and began to roll.

"Tell Carl I'll be along to collect my fee," I said.

"No need, fucker," Gomez said. He threw a wadded bill
onto the grass at my feet. It lolled there in the catalpa beans
and scruffy crabgrass. When I unrolled it there was a picture of U. S. Grant staring me in the face. Carl paid me the
fifty for my day.

Wearily, I scaled the front porch and unlocked the

door I had walked out of over a hundred years ago. My
neck and back ached and the Rockettes tap-danced inside
my head. I stripped off my clothes and stuffed them in
the laundry bag hanging behind the bathroom door,
turned on the shower, and let the bathroom fill with
steam. After a number one, a shower, a shave, and a tall
glass of muscatel with ice, I felt the blood begin to cir-
culate. It was too late to catch the last few innings across
the street, so I decided to fix a good meal, relax, and
play through a few games from the great New York tour-
nament of 1928. Capablanca, Alekhine, Lasker, Nimzowitch. That's the one where a sixty-five-year-old Lasker
faces all the hotshot kids and comes out on top. In the
last game he plays Capablanca, the young classical
Cuban, slicked-back hair and diplomatically balanced
world champion. Everybody expects the Cuban to slice
the old guy like a ripe banana. After all, Capablanca
took the title from Lasker in 1927, the year before, and
was at the height of his power and grace. Lasker opens
with the exchange variation of the Lopez, a slow and
quiet, rather plodding and drawish opening. With sub-
tlety and finesse, the old man wore the temple-dweller
down, and in the end crushed him like a bug. I enjoy
that game as much as any other: Plato teaching Aristotle.

I cored half a dozen ripe tomatoes from my garden and
while garlic sizzled in some olive oil, I diced fresh onion
and green pepper and added them to the oil. Then I added
the tomatoes, some cumin and fennel, fresh bay leaf, salt,
pepper, lots of brown sugar, and a liberal handful of oreg-
ano. Under the cupboard was the last of a decent dago red;
I dumped it in the pot with some water, and then covered
the sauce to heat it. Then I made a salad and washed some
apples and grapes. I uncovered the pan and let the delicious
steam invade the kitchen. Francis must have sneaked in the
front door with me because he was doing curlicues around
my leg and purring like a naked Bardot on leopard skin. I

leaned down and fed Francis a slab of mozzarella. He seemed to like it just fine.

"Francis," I said, "it would seem that Frankie Plummer put in an appearance at the junkyard this afternoon or evening. What do you think? Any theories, old man? How about this? Frankie and Carlotta and Carmen hold up Carl and Bull—and, indirectly, Rossiter—for a shipment of heroin. Frankie needs Carlotta because he can hide from Bull and Rossiter at her house for a while during the time it takes the opposition to get organized. Hell, Bull can't just move in and wipe out his own step-daughter. Bad, bad press. Right? Carlotta and Carmen need Frankie to cop the heroin in the first place, right?"

Francis purred and scarfed down another mouthful of mozzarella.

"So I figure Carl, the old man, hires me because he needs an independent agent to spook Frankie while he stays at Carlotta's place in Riverside. Carl figures Frankie sees someone hanging around he doesn't know, he might panic and run, then Bull and Carl can pick him off. Bull's men don't like me coming around, though. They figure Carl is trying to play the game by himself and leave Bull with the blame that Johnny Rossiter is looking to dish out. Bull's men run me off and the Bull threatens me in order to run the show himself. Bull figures he doesn't want any strange detectives lurking around his daughters when they are holding him up for such high stakes. Maybe there is just no communication between Carl and Bull yet. They both got a big problem."

Cheers erupted from the stadium across the street. Wes Covington probably smashed another rocket against the boxcars past the right-field wall. They should put a sign out by the river: DANGER. WES COVINGTON AT BAT. Have it flash when he gets up to the plate.

"And then there's Carlotta and Carmen. They are lying to cover their involvement in a heroin snatch. I can't blame them there. But, old man, I can't figure out why Carlotta should want me involved with the Bull. To make him nervous? Throw up a smokescreen? Maybe Carlotta plans to use me to make the drop and get her the bread. She needs a go-between, someone both sides don't trust. Therefore, someone like me, neutral. I figure Carlotta and Frankie are holding up Bull and Carl. They probably wouldn't do it to Johnny Rossiter if they want to play ball with him in the future. That explains the sob stories and the kisses."

Francis jumped on the countertop by the sink and sniffed the salad. He found particular interest in the anchovies. I grabbed his yellow bottom and held him under my arm while I poured a saucer of half and half. He lapped it, purring. I poured myself another muscatel and ice. We both lapped, purring.

I stirred the spaghetti sauce with a wooden spoon and watched the red elixir thicken and bubble. Then the screen door in the front room banged and rattled.

A voice said, "Mitch. Are you there, Mitch?" It was a woman's voice and I thought I recognized it.

"Be right there."

Through the screen I saw Carlotta. She had a paper bag in her arms and some kind of plea on her face. I opened the door and she came in.

Carlotta wore blue jeans and a soft white cotton blouse open at the neck. Her middle was sashed with a belt hung with turquoise. Her neck was an exquisite Caravaggio, long and slender and mannerist. She had tied a brown ribbon in her hair, and the broad ponytail fell in an auburn landslide down her back. She was the Rose Parade and Mardi Gras rolled up into one big ball. I realized I stood there in a blue bathrobe with a mustard stain on the tattered lapel, a steaming wooden spoon in my right hand.

"Excuse me," I said. "I expected to get drunk alone, study the Ruy Lopez, and eat some luscious spaghetti and a salad."

"Ruy Lopez was Spanish," she said softly.

"He was," I said.

"He taught that the experienced and efficient chess player should always situate his opponent so that the sun shines directly in his eyes at all times."

"He did," I said drunkenly.

"Was he not also a man of the cloth? A bishop, in fact?"

"He was."

"Did he not also teach that knight to bishop three and bishop to knight five following a king-pawn opening was a most delicate and aggressive opening sally?"

"He took the game right out of the Middle Ages and into the modern era. And Carlotta, sweetheart, if I don't get out of this flimsy bathrobe, I'll make an entirely involuntary and most aggressive opening sally myself." There was an embarrassed silence. "Shit, Carlotta, I'm sorry. I'm getting a little drunk."

She laughed. "I brought some wine. I'm worried, upset, and I need to talk. Have you got some time?"

"Nothing but. I'll be right back," I said.

In the bathroom I put on jeans and a flannel shirt. I combed what was left of my hair and took a look in the mirror. Better than an hour ago, but still a little fuzzy around the edges.

"It smells wonderful," Carlotta piped from the kitchen.

I stepped out of the bathroom. Carlotta stirred the sauce and hummed lightly to herself. Like Carmen.

"There's just enough for two," I said.

I put dishes out on an old round oak table wedged in an alcove between the kitchen and what served as my living room and bedroom. When the spaghetti was al dente and the sauce thick, I finished shredding the mozzarella and grating the Parmesan. We sat across from each other and ate for a while in silence.

The wine was a Bardolino, deep and fine. Even though I was tired and hungry, I was anxious to hear why Carlotta was upset and nervous. Funny, she didn't show it. Cool, like her sister Carmen. That afternoon seemed a million light years across the galaxy from where I sat in the dim yellow light of my alcove, staring across at the silky image of Carlotta.

She looked up. "Have you ever been in love, Mitch? I know you were married once, but it didn't sound like love."

"No."

"That's strange. Why?" She sipped her wine. "You really should, you know."

"Maybe I never met the right girl. Maybe I don't give a goddamn. Maybe it's a question I don't think has much validity in the first place." I was being touchy, trying to keep from digging into her about the lies she was telling about Frankie. Then I decided that she had big problems and it wouldn't do any good to be a rough guy about them. "I'm sorry, Carlotta. It's a question I've been asked before by my aunts and uncles. Every Christmas. Oh, poor Mitch, he's going to wind up like Uncle Vern, living in a little trailer out behind the milking machine. All alone. Never married. I guess it gets me. Sure, sometimes I think about women, about a particular woman, but I just like the way I do things now. It was a while ago that I decided that I would live without the frills that some guys need. Insurance policy, annuity, money in the bank. The hell of it is, I've learned to live with myself. It's not selfish. Just the way it is. I owe nobody, nobody owes me."

"You had love once, in your family. Then you just decided against it? Does it work that way?"

"I never decided against love. Just one kind. Yeah, I had love in my family. It doesn't mean that I decided against a whole lot of other values, you know, like friends, fun, honesty, and the others. It just means I probably can't buy young love and teddy bears and this is forever."

"It's not the same for me, Mitch."

The ball game was over and the ground crew burned just one bank of lights over first base. In that dim reflected light, Carlotta was breathtakingly beautiful.

"You see, I never chose anything. My father was taken away from me, then my mother, and in their place came hatred and evil and there wasn't anything I could do about it. Nothing I could do to stop it or get away. Those values you say you have. They went away."

Carlotta was obsessed. It was making me uneasy. There was a dreadful intensity in her and a hatred that threatened to consume all her beauty and goodness.

Suddenly, she said, "I've sent Carmen away. She left this afternoon and I hope neither Bull nor anyone from the police department is able to trace her. I pray she's hidden."

I finished the Bardolino and poured myself another big tumbler of muscatel. Pretty soon, Francis would have some fuzzy rabbits to play with, maybe some pink elephants.

"Why? For God's sake, Carlotta, can't you tell me what's going on?"

"Not now," she said. "Please." She hesitated. "But Frankie is gone too, disappeared from the house, and I don't think he is coming back."

"When?"

"He was gone when I got back this afternoon. Carmen told me when I came into the house that he was gone. Took all of his things and drove away. I don't know where he went, don't know why. But before he left, he threatened Carmen that he would be back and would hurt her if she spoke to anyone about his stay at our house. For some reason he wants it to be a secret."

"Carlotta, if I'm going to help you, you have got to tell me the honest-to-God truth. Did you ever stop to think I might understand your motives and be willing to help?"

A horrible thought crossed my mind. I wondered if Frankie Plummer had struck out on his own with the heroin, double-crossing Carmen and Carlotta after using their place as a safe house to cut a deal with Bull and Carl. If that was the case, then Carmen and Carlotta had burned a lot of bridges with nothing to show for it. It could explain why Carlotta was so worried now, and why she had sent

Carmen into hiding. And why she was desperate for my help, anyone's help.

"Where is Carmen?" I asked her.

"No," she cried. "Can't you understand? I can't tell anyone. She's my sister and she's in danger." The tears came then. "Why is Frankie threatening us?"

I was beginning to wonder if Tony had his story straight. It was just possible that Frankie copped the heroin and was using Carmen as a shield until he got a deal cut. Maybe he had Carlotta so frightened she found it impossible to confide in me. Then what the hell had I done to deserve confidence?

"Can't you make Frankie and Bull leave us alone?" She sobbed and put one lean hand at the base of her neck. "I'm sorry," she said at last, "I'll stop crying. Then I'll be fine."

"When did Frankie come around?"

"Friday evening. Afternoon. Late."

"What did he say?"

"He threatened to expose us, to harm Carmen unless we hid him." She sighed. "Then Bull told us to put up with him when we talked to him. He demanded it."

"And you discovered him gone Saturday afternoon and made Carmen leave then. Is that right?"

"Yes. And it was lonely and frightening in the old house. So I came here with a bottle of wine, like everything was all right. It's not. Not at all."

I got my chair next to hers and put an arm around her slender shoulders. They felt good. She looked up at my face.

"I just wanted you to know," Carlotta said, "I got Carmen out of the way, away from Frankie's awful taunts and threats and I'm free to deal with this on my own. I just want to see if you can find out why this is happening to us, and do something about it."

"I said I would. Remember?"

"Yes," she whispered, "but I need some reassurance."

She put her arms around my neck and kissed me. "God, I'm so alone," she said.

Feeling her need was like being lost in the jungle, hearing drums. When I carried her to my bed I could feel the darkness opening to swallow me, the whir of a blackened room full of ticking clocks.

In the morning Francis lay curled in the question mark of my legs. But Carlotta was gone.

# EIGHT

I sat on the back-porch rail in my dirty blue bathrobe and smoked the first Lucky of the morning. After the little death Carlotta and I had suffered through last night, I was feeling the kind of wistful sadness that would have made Havelock Ellis wet his pencil. The hound of Mr. Baskerville had camped inside my mouth and done his job—the taste of swill and cigarettes filtered through watery beer, an aftertaste drifting daintily in the Ms, between mendacity and murder.

During the night a grim-sounding south wind had gathered and now rattled and rushed stiffly through the cottonwoods behind me down by the river. A few catalpa beans clattered to the ground. Above the soft and rollicking sea of elms and above the clock tower of old Friends' University, the sky boiled in dirty clouds. It wasn't hot and it wasn't cold, just dry and dusty and windy and the kind of empty only Sunday morning in Wichita can be.

In a couple of months, when the corn and milo fields lay

stripped of grain and drowsy brown in the autumn sun, the crows would come back and roost in the barren elms, transforming them into a strange feathered necropolis. And maybe I'd still be here on the rail. Roosting, just like the crows.

Carlotta made love desperately, in a bubbling and feverish silence that threatened to burst. It never did. "I need you," she said, and I wondered what she meant. If Carlotta had been double-crossed by Frankie and had sent Carmen away hoping to avoid the revenge that Johnny Rossiter would surely inflict, she needed me to fall for her and maybe act as some sort of protection. But protection wasn't my racket and never would be. If Frankie had taken the heroin and cut a deal with Carl and the Bull, it was a sure thing he would be back at the junkyard acting like the only rooster in a bawdy henhouse full of love-starved cluckers. Maybe Frankie had turned over the heroin and split town with a large hunk of change. Maybe he had thrown Carl over and was running the courier business on his own. If you cut the deck like this, then Carlotta came out with a deuce and a death's-head.

One thing was certain. I had been on the case for one day, earned fifty dollars for my trouble, and found a trail that led to heroin, money, and graft. I lit another Lucky and listened to "String of Pearls," which Mrs. Thompson had on the radio upstairs. The wind howled like one of Glenn Miller's trombones. I had been slapped, pushed around, made love to, and threatened. I wanted what every private eye wanted: my freedom and my cut.

I put the coffee on to perk, took a long hot shower, and scrubbed yesterday out of my teeth. I shaved. While I drank a cup of strong coffee I put on a work shirt, old Army fatigues, and my Red Wing work boots. I cleared a space on the kitchen table, pushing aside the spaghetti-stained plates, cigarette butts, and wineglasses. It was hard to believe that eight hours earlier I had picked Carlotta up and carried her to bed. It was something that happened to guys like Spade and Archer, not to Marlowe and me.

I took the Browning automatic apart and cleaned each piece with gun oil and a soft cloth, reamed and cleaned the barrel. I put the gun back together, wiped it down, then loaded two clips. I jacked one round into the chamber, put the gun in a cloth bag, and closed the drawstring. In one of the big, baggy pockets down my thigh I stuck the spare clip and my blackjack. I meant to use the Browning if I had to. When I told the Bull never to touch me again it was one of those childish epithets that a guy better back. Otherwise he looks silly and the guys will push him around on the merry-go-round over at Joyland.

I rummaged through the old streamer trunk at the foot of my bed and fished out a day pack. I put the Browning in the pack, along with a flashlight, two decks of cigarettes and three books of matches, an old bayonet I brought back from France after V-E day, and a dog-eared copy of *In Our Time.* Stakeouts were a boring necessity, so I decided to bring along my plastic pocket chess set and work on my King's Indian defense while I sat and smoked and watched the junkyard. Watched long enough, the spider's nest out at Carl Plummer's might turn up some heroin, and I wanted my share of the action. I also wanted to give Bull Granger a bad day. It was my civic and professional duty.

On the way downtown I stopped by a grocery and bought four sandwiches. I put my sandwiches in the day pack and drove over to skid row to have breakfast. Skid row is two city blocks of bars, beaneries, late-night movie houses, and run-down hotels. The big, red-brick Salvation Army building rises at one end of the row like a Gothic cathedral. Next door, across the tracks, is the ruined marble train station where bums and drifters sleep on benches and mingle with the pigeons. Like all skid rows, this one was bounded by the Continental bus station, the railroad tracks, a Union rescue mission, and City Hall. It was eyed by the police and disdained by the citizens. Drifters—old and young, grizzled and red-faced—leaned in the filthy doorways or hung their heads out the dirty curtained windows along East Douglas. The main goal was sixty cents for a quart of wine and a bowl of chili. The main diversions were dominoes and conversation. That summed up the human condition in the lower depths. I liked skid row and always had the feeling that a streak of bad luck was all that stood between the guys in patched jackets and ragged felt hats who slept in doorways and the fat cats in suede coats with clean fingernails who bunked with blondes out in Eastborough.

I sometimes drank in the Hotel Eaton Tap Room, the dark boozy place where Carry Nation and her gals took hatchets to the bar. I never saw a fight. Down at the other end, the Corral Theatre presented double features for seventy-five cents and if a guy fell asleep they let him snore until they closed around midnight. It was sometimes the only place those guys got to grab a little shut-eye. The Corral had rats and a heart.

I pulled up in front of the Great White Way, bought a Sunday paper from a machine out front, and strolled inside through the big glass doors with gilt lettering. White Way. Snooker. If the Salvation Army building across the street, brick, six-storied, spired, and gabled, with a gleaming white roof, is the Chartres of skid row, then the Great White Way is Les Halles. It's where the locals go for social and political sustenance. A bar and restaurant with the soul of a Fauve.

The Way was a mammoth Victorian hall with a high tin ceiling made of little squares; flowered designs had been worked into the tin by hand and ceiling fans, dangling at intervals, turned slowly both summer and winter. Bright fluorescent bulbs glowed constantly in long banks, illuminating each detail in bone-jarring white and green and brown and gold. Twelve green felt snooker tables and a disheveled row of black domino tables stood in surreal relief against the shiny mahogany bar, the acre of polished mirror behind it. The place smelled of beer, chili beans, coffee, peanuts, horseradish, and cabbage. Take the green felt, the black and brown leather, the gold and silver, cover it with a white glow, add a constant murmur and hum of male voices talking politics, police, snooker, and women, mix in the click of ivory against ivory and slate, and you have the Great White Way.

I sat down at one end of the mahogany bar and ordered chili, eggs, potatoes, and coffee. There just isn't any beer in Wichita on the Lord's day.

Halfway through my first coffee the front door opened and the wind blew in a scruffy old guy dressed in baggy cords and a frazzled work shirt. He was somewhere between fifty and eighty and wore the sunburned, beaten look of a man who did a lot of time on railroads and highways with his stuff tied to a stick in a red bandanna. With a white beard and red suit he would have looked like a proletarian Kris Kringle and when he ordered coffee his voice cracked like the Mojave in August. I watched him over the top edge of the sports page as he dumped six or seven scoops of sugar into his coffee and sat staring straight ahead into the big bar mirror, stirring his coffee. The ear that pointed my way from two bar stools over was covered with hair. The old guy had a straight back and wore a blue bandanna around his neck. He looked at me.

"Howdy," he said. He didn't smile and he didn't pout. He took a brief look at the chili and eggs, then buried his nose in the coffee cup.

"Want some of the paper?" I asked.

He laughed good-naturedly. It was robust and honest. "What the hell would I want a newspaper for, mister?" he said. "I ain't read one in twenty years. The last one I read talked about there ain't no jobs and the land is blowing away from the roots and there's gonna be a war and some Chinese are getting themselves killed."

"Yeah," I said. "I usually toss the front page myself. Stick mostly to the funnies and the sports."

The old guy put his nose back into his coffee. Maybe he had exhausted his fund of conversation in that one-shot social comment. I liked his laugh. I wondered if he would let me buy him breakfast with some of Carl Plummer's fifty bucks and wondered also how to bring the subject to a head without hurting his feelings. I took a gurgling slurp of hot coffee and a mouthful of catchupy eggs.

"You from here or just passing through?"

He turned his head. "I ain't from nowhere. Not since I was twenty-five years old. I left my farm then and ain't been back. Damn bank had it anyhow."

"I was kind of raised around the farm myself. Left as soon as I could, though." The old guy didn't respond. He leaned over his coffee and shoveled some more sugar in. He was eating two or three meals in that one cup. Making it last. "Well," I went on, "if you don't want any paper, how about me buying some breakfast. Hell, I just came into a windfall kind of, and there's no use me keeping it to myself. Need someone to celebrate with before I gamble the shit away. You know?"

It was the best I could do on short notice and I thought he probably wouldn't go for it. The old guy sat in silence, the sound of the south wind rattling the big plate windows, dust spitting against the shiny panes of glass.

Then he said, "I ain't no bum. I don't take no handouts. I'm a hobo."

"I'm sure you're not a bum," I said.

"You say?"

"Well," I responded, "if you were a bum you would have hit me for the coffee right away. Grabbed the section of the paper."

"Well, that's right," he said. "Now a hobo, he don't mind working, but it's just that he don't like being tied down to one particular job in one particular place. He likes to take some time off to think about things and be with his buddies and let the fruit of his labor kind of ooze all over him."

"You want to earn some breakfast and ten bucks?" I asked.

"You serious?"

"I'm serious."

The old guy was Myron Kendall from outside Iowa City, and he left a wife and kid in 1934 to hit the road. He never went home and he never knew his kid. Myron spent some time with the Wobblies up in the state of Washington, but they were dying out then and it was a scramble just trying to make enough to contribute to the stew in the jungles along the Columbia River valley. I ordered a short stack, scrambled eggs, hash browns, and a bowl of chili, and watched while Myron gobbled the mess down. Over coffee I told him I wanted him to watch a house over in Riverside for me and tell me who came and went and approximately what time. He didn't ask me why; he just agreed to do the job.

I said I would pick him up around five-thirty or six and talk it over and give him the ten bucks. He said it was the first time in his life he would ever get ten bucks for sitting on a park bench.

Myron waved contentedly when I deposited him on the bench across from Carlotta's house, the same bench I used Friday night when I met up with Coal Barge and Buddy. As I drove south toward the junkyard along Maclean, past the ballpark, the dairy and lumberyards, then the old county p-farm, I realized I had my own agency now. One old hobo and four little kids on stakeouts. Pinkerton probably started this way.

It was my hope that by plotting the movements of the characters in this melodrama, I could get a line on the heroin. If Frankie Plummer had double-crossed Carlotta, as I suspected, then perhaps I could help her recover the heroin and stick it to the Bull. I had decided to deal myself in on the play. One way to do that was to get information and run a bluff. If Bull or Carl thought I knew where the heroin was, I became an instant big man. Maybe Carlotta trusted me, or needed me enough to deal through me. But the one thing was, I might end up with a handful of acetylene torch flame.

At ten-thirty I parked the Ford on a dusty lane under the shadow of the levee. A scruffy brown mongrel on a tether jumped against a tattered wire fence and yapped at me. I was about a mile north of the junkyard in a clapboard-and-tar-paper neighborhood where the squalor and the chicken crap and the dirty-faced kids get hidden from the general ebb and flow of suburban goodness and light. The levee wall rose about eight feet on a gentle slope and beyond was a ditch about a hundred yards wide that ran north and south around the city to carry flood water from the Arkansas River. It was mostly a kids' playground and unofficial city dump. The Plummer junkyard ran up to the levee wall. it was from the wall that I decided to put the spyglass on Plummer's operation in hopes of finding the heroin and Frankie.

I got the day pack and an army shovel out of the trunk and strung the binoculars around my neck. A couple of shy Mexican kids stared at me from across the fence and I gave them fifty cents to watch the Fairlane. They grinned and took up their posts. I scrambled up the levee wall, down the weedy embankment on the other side, and walked south toward the junkyard. The ditch was dusty and full of blowing tumbleweeds. When I had gone about a mile I climbed the bank and looked over. The junkyard was three hundred yards south and I saw the shack that Plummer called his office. A cottonwood grove hovered above it in the wind and dust. The yard itself was rectangular, full of weeds, sunflowers, and six acres of rusted metal, maybe a hundred yards wide and three or four hundred yards long. The hubcap-encrusted shack huddled near the Broadway entrance, and in the corner nearest to where I crouched on the levee, an old red barn with a mansard roof stood in disrepair. Two old Chevy trucks were parked near the double barn door and each Chevy carried a load of smashed

wrecks ready for the scrap heap. Behind Plummer's shack
the trailer was parked in the open. When I put the glasses
on the shack I could see Abraham the watchdog sleeping in
his wet, sandy hole by the front door. I had forgotten about
Abraham. I scanned the junkyard but didn't see any signs
of life. I didn't see the two-tone Dodge either, and figured
that Gomez and his playmate were saying Mass.

I ducked back over the levee and crawled another fifty
yards to a grove of huge old cottonwoods surrounded by
scrub thicket and thistle. I peeked over the levee, then
crawled into the thicket and opened the army shovel. I dug
a small hole and sat down in it on the levee bank in soft
sand and loam. I placed the day pack beside me and took
out my copy of *In Our Time*. I opened the pocket chess set.
From where I was dug in on the levee bank I could see the
whole junkyard. I was relatively certain that only by accident could I be seen by anyone down in the yard. In another couple of hours the brown basketball of sun would be
completely behind me. Then anyone looking up into the
cottonwoods and brush would be squinting hard to spot a
herd of circus elephants, much less a cleverly disguised
private detective.

In two hours I read about Nick Adams getting shot and
coming home to disillusionment and discontent, played
through three Alekhine games from the Capablanca match,
and smoked enough Luckys to make an ugly little pile of
butts in the dust. Ten moves into a gemlike four-knights
defense played by Rubenstein against Tartakower in Riga
and an intense daydream about licking muscatel from Carlotta's knees, I spotted a black Kaiser roaring through the
front gate of the junkyard, followed by the two-tone
Dodge. The cars stopped in front of the hubcap shack and
Carl Plummer got out of the Kaiser and walked back to the
other car. He stood talking for a moment. In the binoculars
I could see Carl's thin, cruel mouth working. He gestured
to Gomez and his playmate and the two drove to the old
barn, parked, and went inside. Plummer entered his office,

reappeared moments later, then walked to the barn and went inside. I put down Alekhine and Hemingway and stuck the glass on the barn and smoked. Abraham slept in his wet hole. There was no sign of Frankie Plummer.

I waited tensely, not thinking. By now the tumbleweeds blew through the junkyard in clots and the sky was turning darker with dust and topsoil. The sun cut slanting rays through the bubbling air. Then a cream-colored Packard roared past the front gate of the junkyard and skidded to a halt behind the Kaiser. Bull Granger got out. He walked hurriedly to the barn, holding his hat with his left hand and leaning into the wind and the dust. He disappeared inside.

Whatever this troop of Boy Scouts had to talk about took only a few minutes. All four came out of the barn, Gomez closed the big red doors, and they drove back to the hubcap shed. Granger sat with Plummer in the backseat of the Dodge and went with him into the office. They made a nice couple in the binoculars.

Gomez and his boyfriend sat in the Dodge and smoked. Dust swirled around the car and the hubcap shed. A flock of battered crows threaded through the wind and settled into the cottonwoods above the shed. Their feathers ruffled. The cawing and the steady howling of the wind increased the tension I felt. After a few minutes, I put the chess set and book back in the day pack and moved the Browning to the top of the pack, where it would be handy. I took the binoculars off my neck and put them in the pack as well. Where I was going I wouldn't need binoculars. If the heroin was in that mansard-roofed barn, I would see it close enough to put my hands on it. Then I'd have the joker, the ace, and the one-eyed jack.

I got down in the thicket and moved on hands and knees through the sand and scrub. Stickers jabbed my hands. The wind moved the rising dust quickly. At the bottom of the levee slope there was enough of the corrugated metal fence to hide me from the boys inside. I crept along the fence and peered through the gaps. There was no action from the shed. I saw a brown arm popping out of the driver's side of the Dodge where Gomez and his pal were waiting. Evidently Bull and Carl were still talking inside the shed.

I stuck my head through another gap in the fence and pushed aside some sunflowers and buffalo grass. On my left, about seventy yards down, were the old barn and the two Chevy trucks parked out front. Gomez and the boys were maybe two hundred yards away through weeds and rusted wrecks. If they gave me ten minutes I could be in the barn and out with the heroin. It crossed my mind that if Frankie were still holding out on Bull and Carl, they might have him in there too. If so, I would take the heroin and leave Frankie with his tail in the ice machine.

When I'd made it to a hole in the fence just behind the barn, I squatted and held my breath and listened for any sound from inside. There was the howl of the wind and the caw of the crows. There was a squeak and a clang, rusted metal banging against wood. It was steady in the wind and I decided it was nothing holding a gun. I crept down the fence another ten yards and looked at the barn from the other side. I found what I was looking for.

On the side of the barn away from the hubcap shed was a small door latched from outside, the kind of barn door split across the middle and used for livestock and horses instead of machinery. If I could get inside the barn that way, there would be no need to run the risk of using the double front doors and being seen by Gomez. I held my breath and sprinted the ten dusty yards to the livestock door, crouched beside it and flicked the latch. The bottom door gave way easily and I slithered inside, pulling the half-door shut behind me.

The dusty black air inside the barn smelled of hay and oil and paint. Bars of sunlight split the place into black and yellow wedges. I slid the Browning out of the day pack and clicked the safety off. I held it in my sweaty hand. Except for the clanging metal there was an absolute silence. Everything inside seemed cut away from the wind and the tumbleweeds and crows, as if it existed in its own dreadful world. In the dark, I heard something alive and small scurry through the straw and become quiet. My skin crawled after it. My own breathing became stertorous and sweat collected on my chin and dropped to the oily dirt at my feet. If someone opened the big doors, I might have to use the Browning.

Gradually, my eyes adjusted to the murky light. I was crouched next to a row of dilapidated horse stalls stretched along one wall of the barn. Above me, a platform that had once been used to store hay and grain was now filled with engines and transmissions pulled from wrecks. Light from a small, dirty window opposite me illuminated a workbench and a torn-down motorcycle. What got me was the car parked in front of the double doors about halfway to the back of the barn. Unless I missed my guess, it was a dark blue 1955 Pontiac with the trunk and hood and all four doors wide open. I put the Browning on safety and stood up. I dug the flashlight out of the day pack and turned a dancing ray on the car.

It was Frankie's Pontiac. Someone had torn the guts out of it. I walked slowly toward it, keeping the beam of light pointed low and into the ground below the frame of the Pontiac so no one from the shed would see a flash crossing the chinks in the barn walls. The door panels were ripped out and torn to shreds, the seats slashed and pulled from their moorings. Inside the hood, insulation hung like stalactites. The air cleaner and carburetor lay scattered. The same people had gutted the dashboard, and parts from the radio and heater littered the barn floor. The trunk was torn to the metal, and carpeting was stuffed under the rear wheel. It was no use looking for the heroin in the Pontiac because Carl and the boys had already done a good job of that. There was no heroin, no Frankie, and no deal to cut myself in on. I felt the brooding disappointment, the same feeling I had when I thought about the ball I threw into the dugout from third in the bottom of the ninth during the American Legion finals.

I turned from the Pontiac and walked to the double doors and put my eye to a crack. A tumbleweed had blown underneath the Dodge and Gomez was on his hands and knees trying to clear it out. Sand spread like a sheet in the wind and collected in the doorway of the shed. My hands froze against the door. I pressed closer to the crack. Abraham was gone.

It was time to head for the livestock door and make a gracious exit before the torch got too close to my hand. I turned off the flashlight and backed nervously away. Suddenly, I was on my back in the dust and darkness. I gave a small cry. From one of the horse stalls a pair of legs protruded. I had fallen over them. I put the beam on the legs. They wore dark black cotton slacks and white socks stuffed inside black alligator shoes with a gold buckle. I moved the beam up the legs to the torso. Yellow dress shirt and white tie lying askew along the outstretched right arm. Very nice. My light reached the head that belonged to the legs. There was a smooth and untroubled face, a shock of black hair slicked back into a ducktail. Oil and dust smeared the forehead and sand stuck to the pomade in the rich, wavy hair. It was a young face I had seen before, in a photograph of Frankie Plummer taken in high school. Just older and dead.

I took a closer look. Under Frankie's chin a long blue and black crevasse ran from ear to ear, through veins and muscle in the open neck, through the main artery on the side of the throat, severing the gaping windpipe. Someone had butchered Frankie like a pig, and it hadn't taken him long to die his nasty, messy death.

# NINE

I finally stopped breathing like the battleship *Maine*, scrambled to my hands and knees in the dust and oil, and put the flashlight on wide beam. Frankie was still dead. There was a metal water bucket hanging on a nail about three feet over his limp head, and when the the wind gusted through a chink in the wall behind it the bucket rocked and rolled against the splintery wall in a clanking and forlorn funeral dirge. Frankie's shirt was a flashy yellow silk all right, but when I leaned in to take a closer look I saw that the shiny silk became a crusted mess of black on his chest. Shock and fear had pushed blood through the severed veins and major artery in a gush. From the neck down Frankie looked like a Halloween jack-o'-lantern that had up-chucked a load of holiday licorice. Under cow manure, grease from a thousand transmission jobs, and the nameless crud pigeons leave behind, floated the delicate smell of death. Frankie was fermenting. When I touched his hand it was ice cold and limber. I had touched guys like that on

Omaha Beach and I was sure Frankie had been dead for at least one whole Saturday night. It started me thinking.

I checked the car again, this time looking for blood and a razor, not for heroin. There was nothing on the seats or carpets inside the Pontiac, but when I dragged out the carpeting that covered the trunk I thought I could see some stains in the hazy light. It made sense to me that Frankie rode to the barn in the trunk, because I didn't think he had been killed in the barn. At least there weren't bloodstains in the dirt around the car or the stalls that would lead me to believe a grown man got his throat cut nearby, bled four or five pints, then lay down nicely on his back with his legs crossed without leaving anything for the maid to clean up. I crawled back to Frankie and slapped a hand on his rear pocket to check for a wallet. My hand came away cold and sticky and in the intense beam of the flashlight I could see the same crusty mess that was on Frankie's silk shirt. Frankie stood up long enough after his throat was cut to let the blood pulse down his chest and collect in his trouser pockets. It didn't seem possible.

With my left hand on Frankie's forehead I lifted his neck just a little so I could take a look at the damage. The slit in his neck was the color of day-old liver, the kind of smelly stuff I used to take down to the creek on hot summer days to catch catfish with. The path of the wound slanted from beneath the left ear, coursed through the Adam's apple, and wound off and over the right shoulder blade. Part of Frankie's left earlobe was severed by the murderer and the wound was deeper under the left ear and down the left side of the throat. It was a wound made from behind by someone wrapping his right hand around Frankie and slicing him across his throat and down his back. I figured it was someone much shorter than Frankie because the path of the wound indicated that the murderer probably stood on tiptoe and then leaned into his work. When I let Frankie's head down, all the parts didn't fit back together quite right. The coroner could worry about that.

Then I got the shakes. I didn't need Bull and Carl and Gomez waltzing into the barn while I was nosing around in their messy little murder. And if they waltzed in, I didn't want to be on their dance card. Stuff like that is hard to explain down at the sixth floor of the police department while rubber hoses do the doodlebug up and down your kidneys.

I crawled toward the livestock door. Before I got to the door I saw a green Army duffel bag wadded and thrown into the corner of the same stall Frankie had rented for the fall season. It looked out of place, like Frankie himself. I got it open, stuck my hand in, and pulled back a gob of stuff that stuck like wet enamel. It was another five ounces of Frankie's blood. He had been murdered, trussed in the duffel bag, then thrown into the trunk of his own Pontiac. The usual questions came to mind.

I finished sleuthing and crawled closer to the livestock door. Then I heard it. Old Abraham growled a low staccato and pushed his drooling nose and lips into a crack between the lower door and the barn wall. My heart started playing taps in two-four time. A row of white teeth flashed into a bar of sunlight, then disappeared. A nose, a set of teeth again, bumping and pushing against the door. At the other end of the teeth ninety pounds of junkyard dog bristled. I imagined a tackling dummy doused with Old Spice and Lucky Strike tobacco being torn to shreds by Abraham when he was just a puppy learning how to kill snoopers. Abraham left the staccato and started his mean legato, a low growl he kept suspended just above the roasting fires of hell. Then the door buckled, which meant that Abraham had his front paws against the barn. If Abraham decided to bark I would have Bull in front and Abraham behind.

"Abraham," I whispered. "Good doggie." I thought perhaps I heard Abraham modulate his growl into circumspect hatred. "Abraham, it's me. You remember my voice? The guy who works for the guy who feeds you?"

I stuck my palm up the crack in the door.

"Here you go, old buddy. Smell me. It's just old me."
Abraham thrashed himself against the barn door and tore
out an inch of splinters with his teeth. The flurry reminded
me of an old Buster Crabbe short where the cows get stuck
in the Zambesi and the killer fish descend. Then I remembered the Old Spice and the dummy and junkyard dog
training school.

"Goddamn it, Abraham. I can't shoot you." I would
rather shoot a man than a dog, and besides, if I shot Abraham the boys would be down to the barn in fifteen seconds
with their own guns out. It was no way for a slick detective
to make his getaway. "Come on, Abe, Jesus Christ." I
amused myself with the biblical connective. But Abraham
didn't like his nickname, because I could see him through
the crack backing away from the door a few feet, setting
his legs, and throwing himself at the wall. On my hands
and knees I braced myself against the bottom of the livestock door and took the shock. Abraham landed on his feet
and growled.

I got the pack off my back and dug down past the gun
and the copy of *In Our Time* and pulled out the sack of
sandwiches. The top sandwich was boiled ham and Swiss
cheese. I tore the sandwich in half, then slowly unlatched
the wooden bolt that held the door shut from inside. Abraham growled more sullenly. Quickly, I pulled open the bottom door and threw out the boiled ham and cheese.
Abraham pulled backward and thrashed his big triangle
head, then put his wet flared nose down in the dirt and
smelled. Then in one jerk of his bristled neck he took the
sandwich down the hatch.

"Oh, boy, Abraham. Nice dog. You like that sandwich?
Mmmm, boy. Swiss cheese, your favorite. You want another bit, boy?" Abraham growled on, but he had his nose
to the spot in the dust where the aroma lingered.

"Here, boy," I said. I threw out the other half of the
sandwich. Abraham didn't jump this time. He gulped the
sandwich. Abraham and I were having lunch together.

"All right, Abraham. Just for being such a good boy, I'm going to give you another ham and Swiss." I tossed a whole sandwich through the door. Abraham wagged his tail and picked the bread and meat and cheese out of the dirt. He wagged steadily with the sandwich lodged in his mouth. Tilting his head, Abe gave the sandwich a quick *harrumph* and it disappeared into his gullet. I stayed quiet for a minute. Abraham followed his mustard-covered nose to the door and stuck one nostril in the dust. A half inch of weathered wood separated my boot from Abe's nose.

My beloved corned beef and sauerkraut on rye was next. I took it out of the wax paper and held it next to Abe's nose. If Abraham hated sauerkraut, my goose was cooked. I chuckled and shivered at the same time.

"Now, Abraham, my pooch, we're going to try a little more Pavlov. You know Pavlov? Lovable Russian dude." For the first time in two sandwiches Abraham stopped his steady growl and squeaked. It was a sign he had been a puppy before he started tearing dummies to shreds. We were playing. I hoped that *speak* was a command they left out of the junkyard-dog course. I let the bottom door fall against me as Abraham pushed with his head. When the door was open wide enough for Abraham to stick his head inside, I caught his jaws with my knee and held him there. I had the corned beef in my right hand, broke off a piece of fatty meat, and let Abe catch it with his sloppy tongue. He whimpered. Like all junkyard dogs, Abraham was hungry. And I had provided a just and suitable alternative to the Mitch Roberts club-and-bacon sandwich.

"Okay, when I say so, we're going to play a little game of fetch." Abraham was silent. "This fetch game is going to be built on mutual trust and friendship. I feed you corned beef; you don't tear my arm out of its socket, right? Here we go."

I put the day pack around my shoulders again and tore the corned beef in half. In a squat, I pulled the bottom livestock door open and whizzed the corned beef by Abe's nose and twenty yards into the brush and twisted metal wrecks. It came apart and bread and meat and sauerkraut splattered everywhere. Abraham wheeled and dashed after the exploding sandwich. While he played tag with the pieces of my corned-beef sandwich, I strode quickly to the metal perimeter of the junkyard and ducked through a gaping crack. Abraham spotted me and became alert, growling.

"It's okay, boy. I wasn't bullshitting you about the trust. Here." I threw the rest of the sandwich over Abraham's shoulder and into the backseat of a rusted Studebaker. While Abe collected the beef and slurped the sauerkraut, I slithered north along the levee embankment through dust and sand. When I finally saw my car and its two Mexican hood ornaments, I sat in a plum thicket and lit my first Lucky in an hour. I took the smoke down deep.

When I thought about it, what I had in my skull was a theory about hidden heroin that was on a par with electric snowshoes. I flirted once with the idea of Frankie Plummer as a double-crosser, but even that was starting to wilt. What I knew was, I had a guy who steals some heroin from his old man and Johnny Rossiter, then shows up murdered in Carl's barn. The murderer gets behind Frankie without raising any suspicion. This murderer was short, right-handed, and very determined. I smoked a second Lucky thinking about all that, then got into the Fairlane and drove down Broadway toward the junkyard, wondering whether a woman could cut a guy's throat like that.

The sky boiled. I drove Broadway with the top up and the radio tuned to Reverend Theobald Miller of Metro Baptist and his sermon on the power of prayer. The car lots were full of Mom and Dad looking over the new models for next year, already out in September. When I went past Twenty-ninth Street I waved at Joe Stanberry, who ran a motor-car company and sold the only honest used car in town. Joe carried a 198 average in the Wednesday scratch league at Sky Bowl. It didn't matter to me that he made up for his honest cars by cheating at lowball every Monday night in the back room of the Moose Club. I flipped my burning Lucky out the window and wheeled into the junkyard. Under the semicircle of welded metal, I pulled up behind Carl's black Kaiser and parked. Abraham got out of his wet hole and pushed the fur up along his backbone. I wasn't looking for any more trouble from him, just some answers from the Vatican Council inside Carl's hubcap shack. Abraham let me cruise softly past his best low growl and push my way inside the fly-specked screen door.

Carl slumped behind his metal desk, one elbow propped on a knee, his grizzled, gray head nestled in his left hand. His other arm draped over the desk listlessly. The fan in the window behind him whirred and a squadron of flies practiced landings and takeoffs in the dust-riddled air. It was hot and dry inside the shack and the blowing sand and dirt collected in drifts in the corners. Except for Bull Granger, standing with his back turned in a neat blue pinstripe suit, the shack was the same as it had been on Friday when I put in my first appearance. I let the screen slam. Bull swiveled. Carl's head popped up.

Carl spoke slowly. "I told you what for, didn't I?" He snuck a look at the Bull. There was cold finality in his voice, but a speck of pain as well. His eyes were red-rimmed.

"Now Mr. Plummer, sir," I said, "the way I see it you didn't tell me what for. Not at all. You send me out to take a crack at finding your boy and the city's finest run me off. Then I find out it was all a big mistake."

"You been paid," he said. I took the shoulder pack off and cradled it over my left arm. The Bull glowered and the rolls of fat on his neck turned scarlet. His gun would be a police special tucked around the right hip. He'd have to swing open his coat and unbuckle the strap before drawing it. With the day pack over my left arm, I could stick my hand in and grab the butt of the Browning and let the pack fall. In this variation I gave myself odds of knight and first move on the Bull.

"I been paid, yeah," I said. "But I'm a little curious why Frankie would be hanging around Carmen Granger. That's pretty far uptown for a boy like him to go, isn't it?" I was stabbing in the dark, taking swings, trying to make something happen. There isn't a fight unless some guy takes the first punch.

"He was a good boy," Carl said. His voice broke.

Bull said, "Shut up, you fool." Then Bull looked at me. "I think I gave you one warning, didn't I, peckerwood?"

"Now, let's see. Wasn't that down at police headquarters in a small room with two goons leaning over my shoulder?"

"It don't make no difference to me," Bull said. "I'll sit on your shit whenever and wherever I feel like. Now get out of here."

"Not until we have a little talk. Nice and friendly."

Carl spoke. "Abraham," he said.

Abraham came into the shack through a square of screen that was ripped from the flimsy frame. He curled his lips back over his yellow teeth.

"Sit down, Roberts," Carl said. "I'll have this dog rip you wide open if you don't."

"Fine," I said. "Don't mind if I do." I sat in the chair behind me, one not around two days before. Abraham glued his green-and-black eyes to my throat. I had my hand curled around the grip of the Browning, but to get the gun out and to fire a shot that counted while ninety pounds of teeth and fur flew at me through the air would make me slightly better than Annie Oakley's rifle instructor. Abraham sounded like he remembered nothing about a ham and Swiss on wheat, or the lovely time we'd spent over sauerkraut and corned beef.

"Now," Bull hissed, "it's me that wants answers." While Bull spoke I unwrapped sandwich number four, the grand finale: a pepper loaf and jalapeño pepper cheese. I pulled it out of the day pack and tossed it to Abraham. He bounced in the air wagging his tail and got the sandwich into his mouth. He jerked it back. Hot pepper cheese, jalapeño peppers, hot pepper loaf, and Grandma's hottest relish. I've seen grown men cry eating that sandwich.

Abraham wobbled and staggered two steps back toward the screen door while his eyes emptied of hate. He got to his water dish in the corner and lapped at it with his tongue. I could have told him that water on a jalapeño burn was no good. Abraham whimpered and howled and rubbed his nose with both his front paws, finally getting down on the rough floor of the shack and rolling over and over, rubbing his nose and wailing like a baby.

Carl stood. "You poisoned my goddamn dog, you son of a bitch."

"Sit down. Don't worry about your damn dog."

Abraham dashed out the slash in the screen and headed yelping past the cottonwoods for the river. I still had the gun held out of sight.

"Now," I said smiling, "which one is Boswell and which one is Johnson?"

"I told you before what would happen if you kept nosing around, didn't I?" bellowed Bull. He was sweating and the red from his neck swept up to his chin.

"Let's can the tough shit. I want to know what you expected me to find out at Carlotta's house. I want to know what you expected me to learn by tailing Frankie and why you put me off the case before I even got started, before things heated up." Carl broke a little. His face caved in like a coal mine and I couldn't tell the sweat from the tears. Maybe the old man was crying.

"What's going on, Carl?" I asked.

"They didn't have to," he said.

"Shut up, fool," Bull said.

"I don't care," said Carl. Bull spun and backhanded Carl across the cheek. He went over backward in his metal chair, then slowly righted the chair and sat back down, his head in his hands.

"Now, boys. This séance is getting out of hand. But we are getting someplace." I waited in silence. The flies buzzed and the fan whirred. Through the smudged window over Bull's shoulder I could see tumbleweeds flying through sand and rusted metal, cottonwoods waving wildly, the sky blackening.

"All right, boys. Here's how it is," I said. "I got a new client. I want you to listen to me. I don't care that you got a badge and a couple of stooges in the wings. What you really got is trouble with Rossiter and I think I can fix it, but it's gonna cost you."

"Shut up, peckerwood. You don't fix nothing for me," Bull said. "I fix my shit myself."

Carl sat quietly, his head still in his hands. Then the screen screeched open and Gomez appeared. He held a straight razor in his right hand and wore a big grin. I dropped the day pack and let the nose of the Browning rest on his chest.

"First, you," I said. "Then it's your bag of shit Colonel. I promise. What do you say, fuckface?"

Gomez and the Bull shot messages at each other. Bull nodded and Gomez dropped the razor. It hit with a dull thud on the wooden floor.

"Fine, just fine," I said. "Now here it is. You guys got a problem with your last shipment. I really don't care that much, but I know you are having a problem making a deal with the party that is holding you up. Maybe you both need a middleman. Boys, I think I can deal for your stuff, whereas you can't. If I get it, get paid, and get out, I figure I could take a little for my trouble. Then everybody is happy and nobody gets hurt. Well, nobody else." Carl looked up. "I'll say this once. I know your game and I don't care a damn. What I want is for you to let Carlotta and Carmen go. You go back to pushing trash around like a

cop, I make a few bucks, and Carlotta and Carmen take off
with what's theirs."

"No deal, peckerwood," Bull said. "I make my own
way. And you go down. Way down."

"Okay," I said. "You change your mind, you get in
touch. I think you guys need help on this deal. More help
than Carl there can give you. You need someone with
brains because you sure as shit ain't got any."

Bull clenched his fists. They were like hams. I put the
pack over my shoulder and edged toward the screen, then
pushed my way out into the blowing dust.

Along Broadway the day was over for the used-car
dealers. The black sky and whipping wind had driven Mom
and Dad and the kids home to their dinners of roast beef,
mashed potatoes, and butterscotch pudding. I flicked on
the headlights and fired up a Lucky. It was clear to me that
Carl was hit hard by Frankie's death, that the game was
now rougher than he had wanted it. That left me with the
grim feeling that Frankie hadn't double-crossed anyone,
that he had been a clown in a production put on by a major
showman and had gotten himself killed during the first act.
I imagined Carmen's slim fingers and sapphire eyes and
thought how a kid could let himself be sucked into darkness for a lot less. Then I saw a maelstrom of slim fingers
and sapphire eyes. If Carmen and Carlotta were out to de-
stroy the Bull, they were taking along anyone who got in
the way. It worried me to be in the way.

One big raindrop plopped on my windshield and ran in a
grimy rivulet down to the hood, then three or four more
splashed on the dirty glass. I saw plenty of rain like this on
the prairie. Ten minutes of big drops wetting the dust, the
sky turning green and yellow, then nothing. Just a hint of
cool, and a promise of wet. I drove north across the WPA
bridge and looked down at the collection of rusted refriger-
ators, used tires, and automobile hulks lining the river
bank. I felt tired, cheap, and used myself. It took me an-

other fifteen minutes to get back into College Hill and park under the cedar tree on First Street.

When I walked around to Belmont Street I saw Fatso standing by the big elm tree those kids used a a goalpost. He picked his nose and wiped the leftovers on his sweatshirt sleeve. His sneakers were untied and the strings dangled in the grass.

I walked up to him. "Hello, there," I said in an avuncular tone.

"Hello, mister."

"How did things go last night and today?"

"Okay, I guess," he said. "Except those small fry couldn't stay out and they couldn't come back either."

"Well, they're pretty little. Where's your other friend, the guy with the Froggy voice?"

"He gotta go to church on Sunday evenings."

"So you're the last of my operatives on the job?"

"What's that?" Fatty said.

"Well, it's not important. Operative means a guy who works for me. Anyway, you been out here most of the time?"

"Most of the time, I guess," he said.

"Well, what does most of the time mean?" I started to smell four pint-sized rats.

"You know," Fatty whined. "Most of the time."

"Look," I said. "I'm getting dizzy on this ride. Why don't you start from yesterday evening, and tell me how much attention you guys paid to the scene across the street and whether you saw anybody come around."

Fatty backed a step or two. He looked at the ground, drew a lemon-colored booger out of his nose, inspected it, then wiped it on his sleeve. My boat got a little drunk, then the wave of nausea passed it by. I smiled.

"Hey, you're my investigator now. I gotta trust you, see?"

Fatty looked up. "You gonna pay me?" he asked. We now flirted with ultimate issues.

"Of course. Don't you trust me? I already paid you guys four dollars and said I'd be back tonight. Here I am."

"You gonna give me the four dollars more like you promised?"

Fatty put his hands on his gelatinous waist and stared at me cockeyed. For a second I thought about backhanding the twerp. Instead, I dug in my wallet and fished out four crinkled Washingtons. I held one dollar in front of Fatty's snout.

"Here. Take it." His greasy hand snapped the buck. "Now let's start this conversation again. When were you around last night?"

Fatty scowled. "What about the other three bucks?"

"You mean for the other guys?" I asked.

"Yeah. Sure."

"You talk, then I give you the three. You're into me for two already. I'm not gonna cheat you now."

Fatty thought it over. The three dollars ruffled in the breeze like crow feathers. Finally he said, "All right. I was here for a while last night. The other guys had to go in. I didn't see nothing. Now give me the three dollars."

"Wait, wait, wait. You didn't see nothing?"

"Well," Fatty said, "I didn't really see Mr. Granger talking to nobody. That's what you wanted us to look out for."

"Didn't anything go on around here last night? Anything? Anyone go up to the door, stop by, honk? Come on."

"Well, I did see a couple of cars come by like they was just looking for Mr. Granger, but they went away real fast. Mostly anyway."

I decided I hated this little tub. Zits collected in the creases between his nose and cheek and he had the round stupid eyes of a hog. He wore his ball cap all wrong. That was what really got me. His ball cap wasn't broken in right: there was no good break in the bill and the peak was straight instead of rounded. There was no sweat in the liner. Fatty didn't play ball, he just wore the damn cap around.

I said, "What do you mean by mostly?"

"Last night, after you left, we were still playing pass and keepaway."

I interrupted. "You mean you and Froggy played keep-away from those four-year-olds?"

"Yes."

"Terrific."

Fatty took the rag-end of a Baby Ruth out of his jeans pocket and poked the whole thing into his billowing mouth. The nuts and nougat wedged between his pointy teeth and floundered there in a sea of slobber.

"So anyway," he said, "these two cars come up and one drives into the driveway. This lady gets out and gets in the other car, and then the other car drives away. That's it. How about my three dollars?"

"These cars," I said. "What did they look like?"

"You know. Cars. I don't know."

"What color?"

"This one that drove off, I guess was real funny-look-ing. It was kind of small."

"Pink?"

"Oh. Yeah. Pink. It was small, you know?"

"What about the other car? Big or small?"

"Big, I guess."

"What color?" I asked. Fatty evacuated his brain. His eyes flattened. "Dark or light?"

"Dark," he answered. He was losing interest. I folded and refolded the three dollars. He perked up a little.

"So what did this lady look like?"

"Gosh, mister. I told you everything I know. Give me my money."

"Three bucks for one answer. That's asking very little."

I could see the one unbalanced flywheel in Fatty's brain spinning wildly.

"She had real long hair. She was kinda tall. Oh yeah. In

the pink car there was this lady too, but I couldn't see her too well. Oh yeah. Some truck came later and took away the car they left."

I smiled and patted Fatty on the shoulder. He jerked his porky finger away and grabbed at the three bills. He missed.

"My money," he whined. "You said you'd give me my money!"

"Hold on." I stuffed the three bills in my shirt pocket, pulled out a Lucky and got it started in the wind. "Let me give you some advice. Now, see, yesterday you and I made a deal. You come out here and look around for me, then report what you see when I get back. I promise to give you two bucks, half now, half later. Simple. Now you want to hold me up for four bucks. Maybe you don't plan to give your buddies any. Even if you do, see, they didn't do anything to earn it. They took the buck, then did nothing. You gotta keep your word. Do what you say, and if you don't want to do more, then don't. But if you do more than you say, don't come sucking around whining about doing more than your share. You do more than you say, just shut the heck up, and somebody will eventually notice. You get me?"

"You promised me four bucks."

"I'm charging you three bucks for advice."

Fatty stomped his legs. "I'll tell my dad." He turned, then looked back.

My neck caught fire. "Hey, you fat sack," I said. "Go get your greasy old man and bring him out here and we can fry him up for breakfast. Yeah, go get him." Jesus, I thought, what am I doing getting in an argument with some upper-crust ten-year-old on Belmont Street?

Fatty waddled toward his red front door. I turned and walked quickly around the corner to the car and got in. I gunned the engine and sped downtown along Second Street. I could see the headlines: DETECTIVE BEATS FAT KID'S FATHER IN ARGUMENT OVER THREE DOLLARS.

TEN-YEAR-OLD SUFFERS CUT LIP IN ALTERCATION WITH
SLEAZY WICHITA DETECTIVE. Cripes!

By the time I got to the park, a limp sun peeked through
the elms. The house where Carlotta and Carmen lived was
dark and sad. I could see the back of Myron Kendall's head
as he sat slouched on the bench where I had parked him
this morning. I stopped the Fairlane by the Murdock
Bridge and walked through the park listening to the squirrels making their ratcheting noise. Because of the wind,
dust, and threat of rain, the park was empty. Normally
there would be herds of families eating watermelon and
listening to the waterskiers race by on the river. I flopped
beside Myron.

"Hi," I said.

"Howdy, Mr. Roberts."

"How'd it go today?"

"Well, it was pretty quiet for the most part, I guess. We
did have a little action in the forenoon. Otherwise not
much."

"You get anything to eat?"

Myron said, "I ate some peanuts. That breakfast you
bought me is more than I eat all day sometimes."

I offered him a Lucky. He took one and lit it.

"Tell me about it," I said.

"Well, about ten this here tan DeSoto pulls up. There are
three gents inside. It looked like there was a couple of
Mexicans. This one old guy gets out of the passenger side.
Tall, kind of thin, but tough-looking. Flat gray hair. Lots
of wrinkles. He goes up to the door with one of the Mexicans and pounds. I thought that was kind of funny. He
didn't ring the bell or just knock. He pounded and yelled.
Then this young woman comes to the door and opens it but
keeps it on the latch. They start shouting. It was a knock-
down, drag-out mess. She slams the door. The gents go
away. I thought that was a strange Sunday morning hoe-
down. Nothing else happens all day. About an hour ago the
woman comes outside, gets a little pink job out of that shed

there, and drives away. That ain't much for twenty bucks, I'm afraid."

"Nothing else? Nobody else?"

"Nope," Myron said. I folded a twenty and gave it to him.

"How about tomorrow? You want to make another twenty on this stakeout?"

"No, thanks, Mr. Roberts. I really appreciate the offer. I feel kinda strange making twenty dollars spying on somebody. Then, I been working the harvest all August, and I gotta get on with the apples and pears this month. Working too much is bad and that's what I been doing."

"Philosophical differences, huh?"

"Yeah, you could say that."

I shook his hand. "You need a ride downtown?"

"No," he said. "I'll just walk there. Need to get off my can for a little."

"Thanks, Myron. I'm in the book if you're ever in a jam. You come into the Way, we'll shoot a game and swim through a bowl of chili."

He strolled away with his hands in his pockets, kicking his feet at twigs and pebbles. He turned. "I'll count on that," he said and kept walking.

On the way back to the car, I thought things over. Jesus! Carmen and Carlotta delivered Frankie and his Pontiac right to Bull's front door last night. A wrecker dragged the Pontiac to the junkyard where all the boys went through it. That prompted Carl and Gomez to visit Carlotta this morning. I looked back at the big house, dark and somber and gray. The windows rattled and the yellow roses in the yard swirled.

I'd slept with a murderess. Somehow, I thought, it didn't matter at all.

# TEN

On the way home I stopped at Ralph Baum's Burger Bar on Seneca Street and ordered a double chili cheeseburger, an order of greasy fries, and a vanilla malt. They were gone by the time I let myself in through the back door. Francis followed me through a crack in the screen, jumped onto the kitchen sink, and got himself a fresh drink of water from the faucet, which dripped steadily. The south wind had died to an impatient rush from this morning's determined howl.

I looked at Saturday night's dirty dishes piled in a lambent chiaroscuro on the oak table in the alcove, then at the disheveled sheets piled on the brass bed, and felt the sudden desolation and disillusionment of every man who lives alone and goes about the sullen business of making beds, preparing meals, washing dishes, and keeping clean—in the stark face of his own loneliness and despair. Above the rosewood Staunton set, the stern and youthful visage of

Carl Schlecter looked down through dusky wedges of sunlight.

I put my hand on Francis' big yellow head. One of his ears had an inch-long burr knocked out of it and his left eye showed a deep scar.

"Oh, Jesus Christ, Francis," I said aloud. I marveled at another biblical juxtaposition. "I'm feeling sorry for myself again." Francis purred and rubbed his side against my pointy elbow. Then he reversed his ground and rubbed again and purred.

I made a bet with myself that I could persuade Carl and the Bull to deal through me for the heroin I didn't have. I didn't even have an idea where it was hidden. Maybe it was gone. With Carmen. But then, I thought, Carmen was driving the Pontiac just last night when she and Carlotta showed up at Bull's house to deliver their nice surprise package. That meant there was a chance Carmen was still in town and that the heroin was hidden nearby. That gave me some hope that I could convince Carlotta to work through me. If she trusted me. If I could make her trust me.

God, I thought. Carlotta committed a murder in order to promote a fantastic plot to revenge herself on her stepfather and to get what she believes is hers. Bull can't touch her because too many people know about his protection scheme and would put two and two together. Besides, as long as one of them stays hidden to blow the whistle if Bull makes a move, the Bull stays trussed tighter than Johnny Weismuller in a close-up love scene. But I had the sick feeling that the Bull had enough evil in him to pull his own double-cross when it came to exchanging the heroin for money. I could see the Bull arranging an exchange with Carlotta, then killing her when he had his hands on the stuff. When I considered it, my involvement in this mess was intended to prevent Carlotta from destroying herself with her own hatred.

Francis dug his claws into the sleeve of my flannel shirt. "Sure, old boy," I said. I poured Francis a saucer of milk and tuna juice.

After a hot shower, I dug out the phone book and called Carlotta. The phone rang ten times before I hung up, wondering if she was out trying to make her own deal for the heroin right now. Maybe she was up at the Rock Castle talking to Johnny Rossiter. Whether she made the deal with Rossiter or Bull, she was going to need some backup when she made the switch. I couldn't see a guy like Rossiter sitting still for thievery and blackmail while he was supposed to be king of the coop.

When I had the knapsack unpacked and the Browning safely tucked back into my sea locker, I poured myself a tall muscatel and went to the front porch and sat down in the rocker. There had been a day game at Lawrence Stadium and attendants and ushers walked silently in the parking lot picking up Coke cups and hot-dog wrappers. From the players' clubhouse behind a wire fence a tall, gangly, bowlegged kid appeared and ambled to a black '36 Chevy, got a kiss from the summery girl in the passenger's seat, and drove north on Sycamore. The Chevy rattled like a bag of bolts. The kid looked like a lefty to me, some young Warren Spahn dreaming about the big leagues, the glory, and the money. It gave me a bad case of the minor-league blues. The muscatel, the french fries, and the chili gave me heartburn.

After twenty minutes, three smokes, and another glass of muscatel, I called Carlotta. There was no answer.

The wind blew a Braves program over the curb and into my yard. It startled a scruffy black crow, which hopped sideways to avoid the flapping pages. It flapped its own wings in return and cawed, then pecked at the picture of Joey Jay, the Braves's ace. The crow pecking the Jay.

In the middle of peck and a caw I remembered Joe Stanberry standing in the wind and tumbleweeds waving back at me on Broadway. Suddenly I realized what that knowing wave meant. The week before I had promised Joe to repossess a couple of clunkers he sold these two factory types in time to offer them for resale on Labor Day afternoon. It seems he had some end-of-the-season sale going and wanted to offer these two cars at special get-acquainted prices. He offered me twelve bucks a car, and ten bucks for trying.

It seemed like a snap when I said yes because snatching a repo on a holiday is usually pretty simple unless the guy goes out of town. You hit a guy about six o'clock on a holiday morning while he is in the sack. By the time he gets up, he thinks his car is stolen and calls the cops. The cops don't care about a missing junker on Labor Day morning. Sure, a Cadillac is a different story. But not some junker a union man uses to get to work in. By the time Tuesday rolls around, he figures that the bank is probably upset about the three payments he is behind. Stanberry is hoping that the cars are sold on the same day the cops give the guy the bum's rush. When the guy finally makes it over to Stanberry's by cab, Joe says it's the bank's fault. The bank says it's Joe's fault. Then the guy's foreman out at the plant calls and tells him to get his ass to work or he will be scratching fleas at the fucking zoo for a living. He writes the car off and maybe he goes back to Stanberry Motors after two or three paydays and buys the same car all over again. By then Joe has it repainted and the odometer turned back.

I got out of the rocker and headed to the office to review title documents and get the keys to the cars. Joe had left them in the mail slot on Saturday night.

Kellogg Street was deserted. An exhilarating dose of desolation bubbled through my veins. When I reached the top of the Kellogg viaduct overpass, I got out of the car and stepped to the cement guardrail. Below me, fives sets of railroad tracks snaked north through a waste of warehouses, ripped and rusted boilers, abandoned cars and trucks, and heaps of nameless refuge. I blew a ragged plume of blue cigarette smoke into the orange air and looked at the fat setting sun behind the ragged buildings downtown. I thought that Wichita was a goddamn heartbreaker, a shameless woman with her hose rolled around her calves, makeup melted. I turned and leaned my back against the guardrail, arms akimbo, surveying the expanse of clapboard-and-tar-paper squares people lived in, finally to where the elms quit and the broad wheat and cornfields began. God, such a town, laid out in back-and-forth certitude that mirrored the belabored nothingness upon which it was originally built. Religion, family, and profit.

I was losing my friends and growing tired. Reason and luck and sentimentality were no more important than a broken ankle some black woman didn't deserve. It had been six months since I had been to dinner with Andy at his home, and just as long since we shared beer and tobacco over the chessboard and talked about politics and life.

The last time I was there we all sat around the walnut dinner table and found an embarrassed distance encrusting us like cement. The children buzzed like flies at a picnic, upsetting a milk carton, refusing to eat the carrots. Midway into the dinner, the in-laws, stooped and gray-faced, slouched into the room and sat down at the table without a word of greeting. The father stuck his face into my plate and inquired, "What is it?" "Salmon," I answered, annoyed at the question and at the drool that preceded it onto my plate. "Don't like fish," he said, plucking a morsel from my plate and thrusting it in his mouth. "Ugh," he grunted. He extracted the wet wad of salmon, looked it over with the concern of the proctologist, and deposited it on the tabletop. "Don't like fish." The doorbell rang and in swept a frowsy blonde carrying a bushel basket of Tupperware. Andy's wife leaped to her feet and disappeared into the next room with the Tupperware lady. The kids ran away to play. A beaten-down factory couple in cloth coats came in the front door and sulked in the parlor until Andy left the table to discuss a broken toilet in one of his rental apart-

ments. Suddenly the room was empty. The salmon, potatoes, carrots, and biscuits grew cold. I left by the back
door.

I threw my Lucky into the swirling evening, watching
its red glow disappear into weeds and tin cans. I would
help Carlotta make her heroin deal if she would let me.

By the time I pulled the Ford into the lot in front of my
office, evening was in full swing. Thin purple wisps and
blue velvet hung in cloudy fingers in the east and the wind
had died to a whisper. A few eager crickets and cicadas
rubbed legs and cackled.

When I opened the door a smell of dust and ink erupted.
I opened the venetian blinds and let in some hazy light and
looked around. The title documents and keys lay piled on
the floor under the mail slot in the front door and there was
a note from Jake wanting to know if I could go fishing at a
half-dry farm pond east of town on Labor Day. The walls
were covered in stripes of shadow and light. Wispy
mounds of dust collected in corners. Some office, I
thought. Maybe I would do the repos early on Monday and
take Jake up on his offer to fish. No thrill like the thrill of
pulling a five-inch baby largemouth out of a withered farm
pond in the sweltering heat and washing the thrill down
with an ice-cold beer. Maybe even better than sitting alone
drinking muscatel until the game was six innings old and
you could walk across the street to sit in the stands for free.

For ten or fifteen minutes I sat at my desk matching title
documents with keys, taping the keys to the title, making
some notes. The back room was dark and quiet, just the
hum of the refrigerator and the slight wavering rattle of the
screen door in the wind. I got a bottle of Pabst and opened
it, then went out into the backyard.

I put a hand on the rocker to swing it farther under the
trees and away from the sunlight. I saw it. There was a
swish and a sickeningly loud crack, then an emptiness full
of revolving and exploding stars, a demented galaxy of gas
and pure white light. In my forehead one bright flash im-

ploded past my eyes and sped down the ridges of my cheeks. Then a sudden pain expanded and pulsed in my neck. I was on my knees, looking at the blades of blue-grass. The tiny black antennae of a cricket loomed huge in my eyesight. My head and neck burned. Suddenly, another blow shocked my head down. Consciousness lapsed into nauseated darkness. There was nothing left but hooded, episodic dreams.

An enchanted road. Dust spiraling into a pure, royal blue sky. Nuggets in the road the color of shining onyx, the sky as thick and tangible as oil paint. I walked for hours, then days, with a febrile anxiety growing in my chest. I floated, disembodied. Cornfields extended in all directions. Vivid yellow stalks rose straight into the blue sky; green corn sheaths hung down like swollen thumbs. I walked through an impenetrably thick silence. In one fleeting en-counter, two magpies perched on an irregular pole fence, their black bodies and orange beaks wildly contrasted with the yellow and green fields behind them. Goddamn Heckel and Jeckel. They eyed me suspiciously and looked at each other with a mild disapproval. They drooped their malevo-lent eyelids.

In another vision I fished in a sparklingly clear lake. Fireflies danced; willows bent into the turquoise stillness in a sheltered cove. I held an old cane pole and watched a red and white cork bob peacefully on the water's surface, then waver and finally plunge beneath the water. I jerked to the surface a monstrous, growling bulldog, baring its teeth. Its eyes glowed red. Steaming saliva dripped from its vile nostrils. I screamed and felt a human hand on my neck. It was Jake, the barber from next door, and his face was twisted with fear.

"Jesus, Mitch." Jake said with a quivering, tremulous quality. He lifted my head gently and peered into my eyes. I could see the round outline of his face. "Mitch! Oh Jesus, Mitch. What happened?" Then I heard him say, "Harvey, get on next door and bring me some cold towels, the bottle of Listerine under the comb dispenser, and that bottle of brandy behind the cash register." Harvey grunted approval. I heard myself groan.

"Okay, boy, you're gonna make it. What happened? Who did this? This ain't no goddamn accident." I swam in nausea. My body boiled with pain. I heard a screen slam and Harvey was back with the missionary supplies.

"Here, drink this," Jake said and tipped my head to the neck of the bottle. I felt hot brandy in my throat and gagged and coughed. "All right, just take it easy."

Jake swathed my forehead and neck in cold towels and wiped them across my face. He carefully dabbed at my eyelids, then gave me another gulp of brandy. I was coming back to life, but the nausea and pain overwhelmed me. My head felt like one of those pancake heads in a cartoon where Wile E. Coyote gets flattened by a truck.

Like in the movies, I managed to say, "Where am I?"

"You're out in back of your place. I got to the shop this morning and thought you were up kind of early for a holiday. Hell, I just came down to clean up Saturday's clippings; otherwise you coulda laid here forever. Shit, I saw your car but didn't see you inside. I came on in and here you are, laying like some goddamn squashed turtle out on Highway 54. How long you been here? Who did this to you? What the sam hill have you got yourself into, you dumb shit?"

Silvery sunlight danced above me in the mimosa. The air felt cool. "What the hell day is it?" I asked.

"Early Monday morning. Hell, it's Labor Day. You want me to get you a doctor? An ambulance? I think we should, Mitch. You look hurt real bad." He threw the towels over his shoulder. They were covered with blood.

"No ambulance. No doctor. I'll be okay."

"Harvey," Jake said. "Get some more towels. Here, Mitch, take another slug. What happened?" He poured brandy down my throat. The pictures swam, but the outlines cleared.

Harvey returned with clean towels and stood with his hands on his knees and a terrified expression on his face. He was one of the old guys who sat around the barbershop all day. This blood was giving him palpitations. Jake doused the clean towels in Listerine and dabbed at the top of my head. "My God," he said. "You got a damn crack in the top of yer head you could stick a dick into." He dabbed some more. "Christ, Mitch. Here's another crack. You need some stitches real bad, and somebody better look you over. They damn busted yer head open."

I tried to move and couldn't. "Just lay still," Jake said. He rubbed the towel over my face again and I saw it come away red and wet. "You bled a lot," he said.

"Raise me up a little, Jake," I said.

"You sure?"

"Yeah."

Jake put his thick forearm around my shoulders and got me halfway off the ground. Warm blood dripped from my eyelid to my nose. Jake put me down right away. I groaned and felt the pain explode in my head again.

"Here," Jake said. He slid a cold towel under my head and took off my shoes. He loosened my belt and felt my pulse.

"Barbers, you know," he said. "Surgeons of the Middle Ages. Hell, that's what you are: middle-aged. I think I got me some fresh leeches around here somewhere." He laughed.

"Oh, shit," I said. "It hurts like hell when I laugh."

Jake unbuttoned my shirt. He peeled it away from the skin and hair around my neck and when he did I saw it crusted with blackened blood. Just like Frankie's yellow silk. I turned my head into the grass and lost a double chili cheese burger, greasy fries, and vanilla malt. When the retching stopped, I felt cold.

"Get me some hot towels, Harvey." Jake had a cold towel around my neck and wiped the crusted blood away in globs. He shook the towel and bloody flecks detached themselves. When Harvey came back, Jake rubbed my arms with hot towels.

"Oh, goddamn, Mitch. Jesus Christ!"

"What?" I said. "What the hell is it, Jake?" Jake took away his right hand and stuffed the heel of his palm into his mouth. There was a sickened look of fear on his face. "What the hell is it, Jake?" I asked again.

"Your finger, Mitch." Jake spoke in a flat monotone. There was no emotion in his voice.

"My finger?"

"Look," Jake said. He held my left hand in a hot towel and swabbed the top of my palm. I looked. My little finger ended before the first joint and what was left was an ugly sore with a white piece of bone broken and extended beyond the jagged, blue flesh. Blood oozed from the wound.

"Goddamn, Mitch," Jake said. "They cut off your god-damn finger. Jesus H. Fucking Christ!"

I let my head drop into the wet towel. So, I thought, this is what it's like to play hardball with the boys in the big leagues. Mitch Roberts, boy detective. Tries to play with the guys down the block and clucks around in his own blood and loses a little finger. Then I felt a line of pain shoot up my arm and clatter around the elbow. Now that I knew, my left hand throbbed.

"Mitch, I better call the police and an ambulance. This is too much for a barber. You need help."

"No, please," I said. "No police. No ambulance. Just get me up on my feet."

Harvey looked stupefied while Jake and I struggled to-gether. Finally, I was up and we went into my office in a slow-motion shuffle.

"Drive me home, Jake? You keep my car and I'll pick it up when I'm up and about."

"No deal," he said. "First I drive to the emergency room. We make up some bullshit story about how you had an accident, then I drive you home. Otherwise, I call the police."

"Yeah, sure," I said. I had lost a lot of my pluck and didn't feel like arguing.

Around noon I got out of the emergency room with a head full of stitches and a handful of bandages. It seems I was climbing a ladder behind Jake when he let slip a full bucket of paint which hit me on the head on its way down. I fell and grabbed for the gutter but got snagged by the ring on my pinkie. Tore the damn finger off.

"Where's the finger?" the doctor asked. "Dogs ate the damn thing," we said, practically in unison. "What took you so long to get here?" the doctor asked. Jake and I shrugged. The doctor sewed.

That day I stayed in bed, sleeping fitfully, letting the concussion tire itself out. My thoughts whirled in a confused kaleidoscope, but mostly I thought about Carl and the Bull and how they looked at me when I invaded their sanctum and held a gun on them. Then I thought about Gomez and the knife he flashed. It could cut a man's finger clean off. On Tuesday I was up and mad.

It was Tuesday night when my mother and grandma called from the farm. They were hysterical, crying. When I got them calmed down, they told me. A small package came in the mail. They opened it together because the return address was mine. They figured it was a little present. They got the brown-paper wrapping undone and searched the cotton inside. They found a bloody, severed finger wrapped in a note. NEXT TIME IT WILL BE YOUR PECKERWOOD SON'S FUCKING HEAD.

# ELEVEN

That night I sat rocking and smoking. Empty and full of dull anger. It was ponderously hot again and my sweat collected in the folds of the old blue bathrobe. The smoke I blew shimmered in unmoving clouds in the still air. The Braves were winning the championship, and the roar from the stands across the street hovered over the cries of the vendors. "African hamburgers, get 'em now." "Cold beeeeeeeer, getcha cold beeeeeer." At midnight I turned on the Philco to Fred Huddleston's KFH police report and listened to the tin litany of minor disturbances, robberies, assaults, and burglaries.

"At 8:38 P.M. police were called to the Ozell Liquor Store at 3906 West Thirty-third Street South by the clerk on duty, Miss Mildred Sawyer. Some minutes earlier two men entered the store and chose a six-pack of beer from the cooler. When they approached Miss Sawyer one of the men pulled out a small-caliber black revolver and pointed the weapon at Miss Sawyer. She was instructed to empty the cash register and lie down on the floor. The men fled and the clerk called police. She described the men as of normal weight and height, Caucasian. One of the men wore his hair in a pompadour; the other had long sideburns and a tattoo on his hand in the shape of a snake. Miss Sawyer was not hurt. She could not describe the getaway vehicle. The estimated loss is one hundred and five dollars. Police are investigating.

"Thirty-eight-year-old Amos Reedle of 1336 South Emporia reported the entry into his locked garage sometime yesterday during the daylight hours and the theft of a radial saw, two fishing poles, a pair of steel-toed construction boots, and three bottles of whiskey.

"Owners of the Terrace Drive-In Theatre reported a disturbance during the second feature showing of *Teen-Age Crime Wave* at approximately 10:05 P.M. last night. Rocks and bottles were thrown when two cars of high school students engaged in a dispute. Police report that the students had been drinking beer. Police officer Kerry Riggs took seventeen-year-old Milo Weaver into custody. He was released to his parents. . . ."

In the middle of an assault and battery at the Tropics Lounge on South Broadway, it came to me. I knew where the goddamn heroin was being hidden. I knew what Carlotta had done with it. I went to bed then, and slept soundly for the first time in four, long days.

I woke at noon, rolled over in the wet, crumpled sheets, and finally opened and focused my eyes. I stayed in bed, reading the paper, catching up on the pennant races, drinking coffee, thinking about how to keep my anger in bounds long enough to do a workmanlike job on Bull Granger. Heat danced on the venetian blinds and the room was filled with an airless, dusty silence. Then I could hear Mrs. Thompson shuffling around upstairs, changing stations on the radio, humming "Wabash Cannonball" and "Nearer My God to Thee." Tonight, I thought, the Braves played the last game of the season and then the good players went to

Milwaukee to finish September. The stadium would remain empty except for the numb meaninglessness of high school football in the fall. I wanted to do what I had to do in time to catch a few innings of the last game. But that was up to Johnny Rossiter and the Bull.

Just before six, when the sun ducked behind the elms and the air burned less violently, I took a shower and put on a blue silk shirt and my best white linen planter's suit. I looked a little like Dr. Cyclops on Pago Pago. After stuffing the Browning into the day pack, I went out into the plodding late summer heat. I put the Browning in the trunk, started the Fairlane, and drove slowly up Broadway to where the Rock Castle nestled in a grove of hedge and maple.

The Castle hugged Broadway like a hooker hugs a fat man. It was a square limestone fortress in various russet shades topped by two turrets flanking either side of the square. Behind the nightclub a motel court circled a gravel parking lot. A Skelly station flanked the court. The castle, the court motel rooms and their semiattached garages, and the Skelly station were built from the same limestone and took up most of the block of Thirty-ninth Street North. The motel catered to truckers who plied the highway between Nebraska and Texas on their way to nowhere and getting there fast. The castle catered to characters, wheeler-dealers, investors, and men and women on the make. There were plenty of each category to go around.

When it was built in the Thirties the Castle was a speak. When the age of illegal liquor ended it became a roadhouse and gambling den where you could get a steak and a game of craps along with dance-band music. You could still get the steak and the dance-band music, but the gambling had simmered down to a very expensive nightly poker game. I was a nickel, dime, quarter man myself and never sat around the green felt in the back room with the drunken doctors and bankers and professional hustlers. The game was straight, except that Rossiter took five percent of every pot.

I parked and walked through the double mahogany doors. Inside it was dark and cool, and a tingly piano version of "Misty" wafted in the dimness. A tall, thin, and indelibly handsome man with a pencil mustache said, "Good evening, sir." I nodded.

"Will you be dining?"

"Yes."

"Will you be joined this evening?"

"No."

"Very good, sir," he said.

"I'll eat at the bar. Over here with Tom if you don't mind."

"Very good, sir."

Double bars stretched on either side of the entryway. Mr. Pencil led me to the right. I perched on a stool and looked around. Behind me a brass rail divided the bar area from the dining room and dance floor. Square white tables surrounded the polished wooden floor. Brass lamps glowed yellow on each table. There was the inevitable single red rose in a slender glass vase. The room ended in a raised bandstand. Behind the bandstand was Rossiter's office and the room where expensive poker was played. It was early and only a few couples were eating. The place tinkled with silverware sounds and the hiss of silk. The piano in the corner was big and black and played by a woman with icy features and red lips who never went home with the customers. She was very, very good.

"How are you this evening, Mr. Roberts?" said a ruddy voice from behind the bar.

I swiveled. "Fine, Tom. Thanks."

"It's been a while. I trust you are well?"

"Yes. Fine." There was a bloody patch on the top of my head and bandages on the back of my neck where the doctor took stitches. My left hand carried two pounds of tape and gauze. I could imagine how I looked.

Tom Silver's big red and white face swam in an ocean of bar glasses hanging from a rack above the bar. He was the perfect bartender. He spoke when spoken to and otherwise stood leaning against the counter with his arms folded across the massive pad of his enormous gut. The drinks he made were clean and when you ordered call-booze you got what you called. When some woman you were with ordered a gin fizz or a Gold Cadillac Tom made it quickly, correctly, and without the condescending leer of the bartender whose only desire is to stir a jigger of whiskey into a six-ounce tumbler with Seven-Up.

"Waddle it be, Mr. Roberts?"

"Old Grandad with water back, please, Tom."

"Yes, sir."

While Tom poured the Grandad into a shot glass and the ice water into a tumbler, I let my eyes adjust to the dark. Tom sat the drink down in front of me and retreated to the counter, where he leaned back. When my waiter came by I ordered chateaubriand medium rare, sautéed mushrooms, baked potato with sour cream, Caesar salad and French bread.

"Is the boss around tonight, Tom?" I asked.

"Do you mean Mr. Rossiter?" Tom said.

"Yes."

"I'll check for you, Mr. Roberts," Tom said. He walked to the entryway and spoke to Mr. Pencil in a whisper. Mr. Pencil strode deliberately to the bandstand and disappeared into the darkened hallway which ran around the stage. Tom planted himself in his spot. I sipped the Grandad and watched the beautiful ice-woman while she played a very low-down version of "Tangerine." Mr. Pencil reappeared and walked to my side.

"We will speak to you in a moment about your inquiry," Mr. Pencil said. I wondered who *we* were and what *we* were to speak about. A waiter in black brought me my salad and I ate it and finished the whiskey. I felt better and ordered German beer to go with the steak. When it came I drank the beer and listened to music and melted the steak on my tongue.

I was nibbling the tag end of a dish of spumoni when a bruiser the size of Mount Rushmore leaned over the bar. He wore a loose black suit and white tie with a diamond stickpin. You could shave your face in his black patent shoes. He had a thick, sandy-colored face and his eyes were covered by shaggy eyebrows. He looked like Mike Mazurki.

"You the guy wants to see the boss?" he asked. His voice was four miles of highway under repair.

"My name is Mitch Roberts. Yeah. I'd like to see Mr. Rossiter for a few minutes." Tom the bartender walked to the other end of the bar and around the corner. The perfect bartender.

"What about?" Rushmore asked.

"Business," I said. Rushmore blinked and ran a thick finger along the south side of his nose.

"Mr. Rossiter, he's kind of busy. What kind of business you got to talk to him about?" His tone was hollow with no hint of cynicism or impatience. I was not inclined to be flip with this guy for fear he would snap off my arm and use it as a backscratcher. I slurped another gob of spumoni, took the whiskey and swirled it in front of my eyes. I looked at Rushmore through the liquor.

"This business," I said, "is private. Very private. Mr. Rossiter gives me one minute and I guarantee he will want another fifteen on top of it."

"Whadda you selling? Encyclopedias?" Mr. Pencil peered around the corner from his spot near the front door. Tom edged back. Three tables over there was laughter and the ice-woman played "Take the A-Train."

"Tom," I said, "please get me a pen." Tom reached in his white jacket pocket and produced a gold fountain pen. I took it and wrote on my cocktail napkin: *I know where the shit is hidden. Mitch Roberts.* I folded the napkin and handed it to Rushmore. He unfolded it, read it carefully, then returned and walked into the darkness behind the stage.

The waiter cleared my dishes and Tom returned to his spot. "Will there be anything else?" he asked.

"How about some plaster of Paris?" Tom smiled. I finished my whiskey and waited. In five minutes Rushmore walked briskly from the darkness. He was followed by a dark little man in blue pinstripes with a white carnation at his lapel. His ears looked like kites. The two men got up to the bar and stood around me in a half circle of quiet stares. The dark man had a big hook nose.

Finally Hook Nose said, "Come on." I got up and the three of us walked through the gate in the brass rail and back to the darkness behind the bandstand and into a narrow, heavily draped corridor. I knew the poker room was at the end of the corridor. Halfway down was another door on the left. Probably Rossiter's office. Rushmore put his hand on my shoulder.

"Hold on, cowboy," he said. He shoved me gently and I stopped with my back to the draped wall. "We're just gonna check you over. No problem with that, is there?"

"No problem," I said. Rushmore stood two steps back while Hook Nose patted me under the arms and down the legs. He turned me and went over my back pockets and down the back of my calf.

"Let's go," Hook Nose said. Rushmore knocked on the door. A voice inside said, "Yeah," and we all went in.

Rossiter's office was a fifteen-foot square carpeted in white shag. The only light came from a lamp that cast a circle of yellow on the glass top of the steel and glass desk. Rushmore sat in a beige couch against one wall and Hook Nose leaned against a shiny wet bar on the other side of the room.

Johnny Rossiter sat behind the glass and steel in a black tuxedo. He had the body of Fred Astaire and the high forehead and slicked-back hair of Valentino. His hands were graceful, the fingers delicately small. He was eating a small filet and green salad. Rossiter didn't look up or speak. He just ate his filet and sipped at a goblet of wine. When he had finished, he carefully wiped his mouth and hands with a monogrammed linen napkin, lit an English Oval, and raised his limpid eyes.

"Sit down," he said. His voice was precise. I sat in a leather chair at an off-angle to the front of the desk. Hook Nose removed the dishes from the desk and piled them on the wet bar.

"You've had an accident," Rossiter said.

"You could say that," I responded. "It's been a very tough few days."

"You're Mitch Roberts. You're a private detective with not a lot on the ball and you send me a note like this." I stayed quiet.

"Wine?" he continued. Hook Nose gave me a goblet and splashed Margaux into it. It had more nose than the muscatel. I was tempted to make a joke about nose for the little guy's benefit.

Rossiter pasted his droopy eyes on mine. "You'll want to explain in certain terms the meaning of the note and the purpose of your visit. Don't embellish and don't lie. Come to the point and I will make some kind of judgment."

I sipped the wine. "A few days ago Carl Plummer hired me to tail his son and gave me directions on how to find him. It seemed odd at the time and the deal fell through when Plummer took me off the case right away. By accident I found out that Frankie Plummer stole something that belonged by rights to Johnny Rossiter and that Carl was upset. Lots of people were upset. It didn't mean much to me at the time. But then I ran into a pair of young women who interested me and I learned that these two might have some knowledge of where the stolen merchandise might be. By that time the principals were anxious to discourage me from making further inquiries, from learning any more professional secrets. I can't blame them. I would have felt the same way. So these people arranged for me to have an accident. But I'm not discouraged. On the contrary. I am mad as hell. Now, I sat around for a few days letting the knots on my head unravel and something came to me. What came to me was where the merchandise was hidden. Just deduced the goddamn answer out of thin air. But I'm sure I know and I'm sure I'm right."

"What do you propose?" Rossiter said.

"I return the merchandise to you. You pay me a finder's fee."

"You think I should buy merchandise that belongs to me already? Merchandise I bought and paid for? What kind of businessman would that make me, Mr. Roberts?"

"I'm a businessman too. I want ten thousand. If you don't like it, get the ten thousand from the people who lost the merchandise in the first place."

"What assurance do you have that I won't simply have you killed when you return the merchandise?"

I raised my glass. "I'm not worth it," I said.

Rossiter leaned back in his chair and smiled. "When can you deliver this merchandise?"

"Tonight." I paused. "There's one other thing. These two women. When I return the merchandise, they have to be left out clean."

Rossiter inhaled some English Oval. "I see," he said. We sat in silence. I knew I was taking a chance trying to sell Rossiter on the idea of paying for the return of heroin he considered his own. But I decided that if I made the price tag low enough he just might do it to avoid problems. And if I made the price tag high enough he would feel my services were valuable.

"We close at three A.M., Mr. Roberts. I'll expect to see you before that time. There is enough cash in this room to cover your expenses. If you show up with the merchandise, I'll pay you and send you on your way. I'll even ignore the women of whom you speak. You will be away clean, as you say."

"All right," I said.

"On the other hand . . . Should you fail to keep your appointment with me I will have you tortured and then killed. Is that clear?"

"What if I'm wrong?"

"Then," Rossiter said, "you will be dead wrong. Is it clear?"

"Clear."

"Good then." Rossiter stood and extended his narrow hand. I shook it. Rushmore and Hook Nose joined me for the walk down the corridor. They left me at the bandstand and headed back down the darkened passage. Hook Nose turned. "Good fucking luck, punk," he said.

I walked back to the bar. Tom leaned in his spot. There were more couples at the tables. Tom stepped forward. "It's been taken care of, Mr. Roberts. Thank you very much."

"All right, Tom. Good." I dug in my wallet and got a five and put it in the tip bowl.

"Thank you, Mr. Roberts," Tom said. I walked past Mr. Pencil and through the mahogany door.

Outside, a few whimsical stars dusted the eastern horizon, already streaked cerulean blue. A slow freight chugged north. The fireman waved a red lantern.

In the wavering twilight I drove south on Broadway, past secondhand stores, junk shops, Mexican diners, and used-car lots. When I got home to Sycamore I changed into a pair of blue jeans and a dark, lightweight turtleneck. I put the blackjack in my back pocket and the Browning in the front seat. Then I drove over to College Hill and parked under my trusty cedar tree. I felt grim as a Goya.

The night was blowsy and the elms paraded in a sibilant rush, waving their leafy arms and creaking in the steady south wind. Light from the copper lamps on Belmont streaked the darkness, the rays and shadows colliding in an eerie embrace on the lush, dark lawns of the rich. Across First Street the door to a two-story Ozzie-and-Harriet stood open, and the blue light of television oozed onto the sidewalk. Then the sound of canned laughter broke the windy silence. A dog barked. My heart did the tango and I sat smoking, thinking with cruel remorse about the night I spent with Carlotta and about the sad-faced lady on the desk in her house in Riverside. I suddenly felt a longing for the life of quiet and anonymity I had lived for so long. It was funny. I started thinking that tonight was the last night of the minor-league season. Guys like Joe Torre, Juan Pizarro, Joey Jay, Hammering Harry Hanebrink, and Carl Willey and Wes Covington would be gone forever from this square, brown prairie town. They would make it to the bigs. Shit, I thought, I should be there to watch them go.

I felt anger and fear and despair and when I finished my smoke, I locked the Ford and crept into the alley that ran along the back of Colonel Granger's Tudor outhouse. Somebody's idea of a ragman scarecrow startled me in the gloomy shadows and I shivered respectfully at what went through my mind.

Bull's big house was dark and empty-looking. I huddled behind the garage, away from the thin mist of light that escaped from the bulb over the double doors. Through a dusty window in the back wall of the garage I could see that Bull's creamy Packard was gone. I held my breath and peered into the windswept ink of the backyard. There was an empty birdbath, a couple of lounge chairs, a row of thick cedar hedge shielding the yard from the neighbors, and no sign of a snarling Doberman. I picked up a stone from the alley and tossed it toward the back porch. It clattered against the flat stones. No barking, no snarling, no lights, and no sirens. The alley was a jungle of hedge, vine, and mulberry, and I didn't think any of the neighbors could see me from their kitchen windows. Out on Douglas only a few cars passed. I hopped the picket fence and silently pushed my way through the side door of the garage and went inside to wait for the Bull. It was hot inside and sweat soaked my clothes.

With the door shut behind me, I stood still and looked

around, adjusting my eyes to the new darkness. The garage was empty. Silent and sterile as a Southern Baptist dance hall. There was none of the usual suburban stuff like scattered tools, hoes and rakes, toys, old barbecue sets, coils of hose, and bicycles. Neat rows of pasteboard boxes rose at the back end; along the south wall at my elbow a neat squirrel cage held ordered arrays of hoes, rakes, trimmers and mowers. There was a gardener at work. Maybe a servant or two. Certainly no evidence of some harried Dagwood in a holey woolen sweater raking the lawn, throwing his tools in a scattered pile in the corner before playing catch with his bucktoothed kids. A faint oil spot marked where Bull parked the Packard. From the position of the spot I could tell that Bull pulled his car into the north side of the two-car garage and got out with only a few feet to spare between himself and the north wall. I sat in a dark corner to the left and behind where Bull would stand when he got out of the driver's door. If there was a passenger with the Bull when he came home, my plan wouldn't work. But that didn't seem likely.

I squatted in that dim corner for thirty minutes. When bright car lights broke the plane of darkness, I pulled the blackjack out of my back pocket and pushed the Browning deeper into my belt. The Packard idled. My heart accelerated.

The Bull grunted, then heaved up the double garage doors and got back into the Packard. The big car rolled into the dark garage past where I squatted in the corner. It purred and puffed carbon monoxide into my face. I could see the outline of Bull's big neck where it bunched up in rolls under his felt hat. He was alone. After a pause, he shut off the motor and opened the door. When he got the door open and one leg out I was up from the darkness taking two quick strides toward him. He said something like, "Whaaaa..." before I clipped him behind the right ear with the fat end of the blackjack. He yowled and grabbed at the spot.

He swooned and his hat dropped to the floor. I pushed his face down and back until he was prone on the front seat of the Packard, an abandoned whale on the camel-hair beach. The car's yellow overhead light revealed a fat, obscene face, floppy jowls hanging in arches around the chin, bushy eyebrows growing like radioactive lichens above his piggy eyes. His chest heaved and I could see that he was conscious, but barely hanging onto the edge of a whirling galaxy. He held one porky hand below his right ear and groaned.

"Goddamn it," he said in a bewildered growl. "What the fuck is this?"

I got his thick left leg untangled from his suit coat and draped it over the right leg and under the ivory steering wheel. Then I grabbed the heavy car door with my left hand and shut it gently on the ankle of Bull's right leg. He eased up on his elbows and looked at me with a confused scowl. The window was down and I could see a look of hatred and sickness simmering in the dim light.

"You," he said.

"Hi." My hands shook. I stuffed the blackjack into my rear pocket and hauled out the Browning. My bandaged left hand did nothing but hurt.

"This bullshit is your last trick, son of a bitch," the Bull said. He was up off his elbows and had one hand on the steering wheel desperately trying to get his balance. I poked the nose of the Browning inside.

"Get back down." The Bull glared at me, then looked the Browning up and down with an air of modest disrespect.

"You won't," he said. "You ain't got the fucking guts."

"Try me," I said. The fear was gone from me and now I operated in the airless region of pure hatred. I lodged one foot against the garage wall and gave the car door a quick shove against Bull's trapped ankle.

"*Aaagghhh,* Jesus Christ!" I pressed my full weight against the door and bounced it with my shoulder. The Bull gurgled fish sounds and dropped back to his elbows, then onto his back and put his right forearm over his eyes. In an instant he was up, lashing out with his right hand for my face. He missed as I ducked and levered the door against his ankle. Bull disappeared back down to the seat.

When I looked over the window edge the Bull struggled with the gun at his hip.

"Don't," I said. I leaned inside the car and pointed the Browning at his bloated belly. "Unhook the belt buckle and keep both hands in front. Then let the ends of the belt go free and slide the belt away from you and hand me one end. Do it slow and easy. If you don't I'll shoot you someplace and stop you and maybe I'll kill you by accident."

"You won't get away with this. You're a dead son of a bitch." The Bull finished his promise, then slowly unbuckled his belt. It came away and he leaned up and I got one end of the belt in my bloody bandage and pulled belt and gun away from the Bull.

He leaned back on his elbows. "What the fuck is this?" he asked again. There was a hint of vulnerability seeping through the hard guy.

"Listen," I said. "Be quiet and listen. You make any sound and I shoot you. Fucking breathe like you're gonna yell and I'll put a bullet in your goddamn forehead." The Bull started to speak, then relaxed. "You and your goons gave me a hard time last week. I told you then. Do it again and I'd kill you." While I spoke I increased the pressure against the car door. Bull broke a heavy sweat and his face contorted. He made no sound. "What it is, Colonel, is a fucked-up hand and a bashed-in head and the finger you sent my old lady."

"Hey, what are you talking about? I don't know about any of this. What I know is you got your nose in deep, coming around making deals like you're trying to make. I don't know who burned you. It wasn't me. I will next fucking time."

"Fine," I said. "You're taking the fall for Carl or Gomez

or his chicken-taco buddy." That was when I backed off the door and relaxed. Quickly, I slammed it shut again as Bull tried to pull his ankle out. There was a sharp crack and Bull croaked in pain. I bounced the door against the ankle. I heard skin tear and two or three more cracks.

"Oh God. Oh God. Damn it." Bull pounded a meaty fist on the dashboard. I jammed a foot on the top of Bull's instep and pushed on it with all my weight. The ankle gave with a shrill pop and waved at a demented angle. Bull gasped. He stared up out of the yellow mist.

I said, "That one wasn't for me. That was for the black lady down at police headquarters."

"Look," Bull rasped, "you want to make a deal, you got it. I'll give you part of the action. Frankie's dead. You know that? You can take his place. We need a tough guy. There's some dough in it." Bull's face was red and twisted.

"No deal. Let me tell you what's happening to you. I'm snapped out, see? Wacko. Psycho. Fucking crazy. I see guys like you shove people around all the time, guys in big fancy cars and felt hats and heavy coats. They got the dough and they got the diamond rings. Hell, maybe that's okay. I don't give much of a shit about that. But you. You just gotta push people around for the hell of it. Maybe everybody pushes somebody around once in a while. But it's guys like you got no excuse to exist. You make everything smell like shit."

"You fucking asshole," Bull said. "Shit like you is made to be pushed. You think you're any better? I know about you. Fucking repossessing some guy's car, sucking up cheap jobs and booze. You're in the same shit we're all in, gunsel. You just ain't got as much of the action."

"Then," I said, "there's Carlotta and Carmen and the woman you forced out of the police station window without a net. That's something extra that works on me."

The Bull was tough. I had to hand it to him. He didn't beg and he didn't whine.

"Fuck it then. Maybe you're right. It's just revenge,

Colonel. That's all. It's for me because I hate your fucking guts and you backed me into a corner and slapped me around, then cut off my goddamn finger."

"You're crazy," Bull said.

The bullet went into the middle of Bull's zipper just below where his belt had been. It made a sickening thud and Bull's body convulsed with shock, then shuddered. Then I heard the explosion of powder. Bull lay spread-eagled on the camel-hair seat of the Packard, a circle of dark blood radiating from the small blue bullet wound, soaking his pants. His right hand quaked like a wet sparrow on the floorboard and his eyes twitched shut. A blue swath of cordite rose to the tan headliner and hovered there.

If any of the neighbors had heard the gunshot they would be talking it over right now, trying to decide whether it was a backfire, a firecracker, or a 9mm Browning automatic. There was a fifty-fifty chance that some housewife in mudpack and curlers was dialing the cops to report a strange noise. But there was an equal chance that some husband was saying shut up and go back to watching TV. To me it was worth the gamble to watch Bull die.

"Oh God, help me. Help me." Bull's voice trembled. "Oh please," he said. I watched the red circle expand and collect on the rich camel-hair front seat. Bull grabbed his stomach in both hands and tried to hold the blood and guts inside. Somewhere down there a slug had ripped into his intestines and rattled around. Bull had his head down and his chin back. "Get me a doctor. Get me a doctor. Call ambulance," he whispered. Blood bubbled from his nose and the corners of his mouth. "Why?" he said.

The Bull coughed wildly. He brought his hands away from the wound. They were covered with slick blood. "It hurts," he said. I stuck the Browning into my pants and closed the car door. When I looked back inside I saw clots of blood on Bull's chest where it erupted from his mouth and nose. Bull held his legs in a V, the broken ankle swollen grotesquely out of his wingtips. Then he seemed to relax, and with one soft cough he was quiet.

I got out quick and walked through the alley. It was a zombie who drove west into Riverside Park, under the black wavery shadows of the crow-shrouded elms. And when I stopped, I saw that Carlotta's Victorian was dark.

# TWELVE

I sat on my park bench and watched Arcturus shimmer red through a purple cirrus web. Behind me, the bears paced and got up on their hind legs to stick their noses through the black iron bars of their cages, sniffing patiently for the popcorn and crackerjacks that kids threw. Well, I knew how they felt. A frightened dancing bear with cracked skin and a short life expectancy. But I was emptied out. The sweat and the trembling and the adrenaline disappeared down a hole of relief and fatality. I had killed a man in cold blood for my own reasons and there was nothing left of the panic and anxiety, nothing left of the pride and vanity that made me point the Browning at Bull's fat gut and pull the trigger and feel damn happy about it.

I relaxed and took a lungful of smoke and looked at Carlotta's house, thinking about her body and the way it felt Saturday night when I made love with her. She was a beautiful woman and I wanted her, but that was all behind me. I was going to walk across the street and get the heroin and sell it back to Johnny Rossiter. I figured that Carlotta would get what was coming to her and I would too. So had the Bull. If the heroin was gone, then I would wait and let Rossiter take his best shot. It was a gamble with larger stakes than I wanted. But it was my gamble and I had to see what the cards said.

I got my Army shovel out and walked in the wind and darkness across Nims. I jumped the curb, then hopped over the picket fence and landed in the peonies and roses. In front of me was the Texas Beautiful, full of blooms with no scent, lovely and dimensionless. On my hands and knees I felt the loose earth beneath the rose. It had been turned. When I put the shovel down the blade went in easily. I scooped out three shovelfuls, then dug with my hands until I struck hard earth. My heart raced. If the heroin wasn't under the bush I might as well reserve a plot at Maple Grove and start composing an epitaph. HERE LIES A STUPID, VAIN PRIVATE DETECTIVE WHO MEDDLED IN SHIT LARGER THAN HIMSELF.

The wind was hot. The elms waved wildly. From the darkness of the old porch I heard her voice.

"It's not there," she said. The sound was lost in the filmy whooshing wind. I gazed into the shadows, then stood up and dropped the shovel. By the time I got halfway to the porch I saw her in the wavering shadows by the old swing. She wore something white. She looked like a ghost.

"No," I said to the shadows. "I really didn't suppose it would be."

"I'm sorry, Mitch," she said in a whisper. I walked up the porch steps, letting the surprise and disappointment sink in. Jesus, I thought, what am I going to do? Am I going to let Rossiter and his muscle push my face in the dirt and pour cement in my shoes? Will the fish start with my eyes and work my asshole for desert?

I got to Carlotta, stopped, and watched the wind blow her hair in a stream around her shoulder. Her cotton blouse was open at the throat and revealed her long, brown neck.

She had on jeans and sandals and she smelled faintly of musk. When she stepped from the shadows I saw she had been crying.

"Are you hurt badly, Mitch?" she asked. She put her hand on my cheek, then wrapped both hands around my neck and held me silently. She cried. I could feel her tears on my neck.

"No, not badly."

"You'll be all right?" She put her cool cheek against mine and kissed me, then led me to the swing. We sat down and stayed quiet. She put her head on my shoulder. The wind blew her hair across my forehead.

"I'll be all right. He got my hand pretty bad, put a couple of knots on my head. He didn't figure on that being my least vulnerable territory."

"I'm so sorry. I'm so sorry, Mitch," Carlotta said. She sniffled. The streets were empty and the park deserted. I kissed her mouth.

"Do you know?" she asked me after the kiss.

"I do. I think I do." Carlotta wiped the last tears away from her eyes with the back of her hand. She gave me a halfhearted smile.

"You don't hate me?"

"God, no, Carlotta. I don't know you very well. But I don't hate you. What you did, well, I can understand it. Maybe I can't judge you or anybody else for feeling like you do, for wanting to hurt somebody badly enough to kill in the name of the feeling. For revenge. In the name of some principle or other." Carlotta had her head on my shoulder again. As I spoke I watched the bears pace in their cage.

"How? How did you find out?" she asked me at last.

I kissed her. "I got into the barn out at Plummer's junkyard. They had the Pontiac towed there when you left it at Bull's house on Saturday."

"You know about that too?"

"Professional stakeout. Operatives under the pillows, in

the pantry. Operatives to the left, behind the hour hand, in your hubcaps."

"We had to. We had to kill him."

"I know. Which one of you did it? How did you manage?"

"Oh God," she said. "You won't hate me?"

"No, of course not."

"He was hideous. He pranced and preened and he was such a child. He was vain and arrogant and we decided we could use him. It wasn't hard because he never questioned his power over women, his attractiveness. He really thought he was irresistible. We never intended to kill him. You believe that, don't you?"

"Yes, I believe you."

She shook her hair free. "He wanted to get away from being just a gofer for his father. He wanted to get some real action. It wasn't until he approached Carmen at a party Bull gave that we had any idea that Bull provided protection for Rossiter. We knew he was crooked, that he got money from some source, but we both thought he just protected pinball-machine owners, bartenders who stayed open late, poker games, prostitutes. We knew he was capable of any sort of evil, but we didn't know about Rossiter." She stopped and took a deep breath. She ran her fingers over my bandaged hand. "Are you in pain?"

"Some. Not much." I got out a Lucky and sat smoking.

"It was Frankie's attention that started us thinking. We were desperate. He came to the house and hounded us, making ugly remarks, swaggering. The Bull enjoyed our suffering. He knew Frankie did it, knew how we hated him. Bull enjoys pain, though, enjoys other people's pain, he enjoys watching, being responsible. And so he encouraged Frankie. Carmen was terrified, of course. One night Frankie was drunk and started talking about his business. He called it that. His business. We could tell that his business involved Bull and Johnny Rossiter, and finally, when he was very drunk, and making just a little sense, he told the whole story. How Carl ran heroin in from Mexico. He did it by hiding it in shipments of scrap metal loaded on trucks and driven from Mexico to Wichita. The junkyard was a good cover and Rossiter used it well. The Bull protected these people and was well paid. I suppose Frankie thought that the Plummers should have more for what they did. He kept saying he was going to crack Rossiter. He had a scheme. It was then he told us he was planning to hold Carl up by disappearing with a shipment, then muscle his way into the business. That's all it was to him. Just a way in his drunken dreams to become bigger than he was. It never would have worked. Rossiter and his people would have broken him, made him talk, and that would have been the end of Frankie's dreams. The whole scheme was probably just drunken talk. He could have gotten up in the morning and the idea would have been gone and he would have stayed Frankie Plummer. He kept saying he was no small fry. They couldn't keep treating him that way."

"So," I said, "you showed him a way to make his scheme to steal the heroin possible."

"Yes." A quarter moon danced in the elms, its light silver. "We calmed him down and showed him a way to make his dream come true. We told him he could steal the heroin and use us for protection. The Bull can't allow his own stepchildren to become involved in a thing like this. It becomes perilous for him. What if the papers find out? What if the Chief and all the boys who know about this protection racket all of the sudden won't stand behind Bull anymore? No, we made Frankie see that if we all participated in the deal Bull would have his hands tied, that Rossiter wouldn't just barge in and start hurting people. Frankie liked it."

"What would you do? Did you know?"

"Ruin Bull. It's all we ever wanted. We wanted him ruined the way he ruined our mother. We hated him. I don't think we knew exactly what we were going to do when Frankie decided to steal the heroin and come here to hide.

We knew we had a few days before Carl and the Bull and
Rossiter all got together to plan something. We knew we
had to do something in that time. In a week, maybe less,
things would start to fall apart. And then we didn't trust
Frankie. It turned out that he planned to sell Rossiter the
heroin and cut us out. If he did that, our idea for ruining
the Bull would be meaningless. We decided to kill him. It
seemed the only thing to do. You understand?"

I nodded.

"We were desperate. At our end. And we were frightened of the Bull. Afraid he would make some decision to
burst in and terrorize us. To throw things over. And so we
decided to kill Frankie. He was already dead when you
came here on Saturday. He was upstairs, dead."

"How? How did you do it?" Carlotta closed her eyes.
"I'm sorry. I want to know. I can tell you why if you
want."

"No. It's all right. You should know everything." Carlotta stood and walked to the porch rail and looked into the
night. She turned, sat on the rail, and put her hand to her
forehead. "It's so hot," she said. "The wind and the heat, it
makes me feel restless." I leaned back in the swing.

"He was shaving," she said. "That's funny, isn't it? He
was shaving and he cut himself badly." There was nervous
hysteria in her voice. I got up and held her and stroked her
hair.

"It's all right. Don't say anymore."

"I want to." She gathered herself. "Carmen got behind
him. He was singing. She cut his throat with a straight
razor. It was horrible. There was a hideous gurgle. The
blood was awful." I felt her tremble.

"He stood," I said. "How could you handle him?"

"I was there. In the next room. I watched while Carmen
went to him and watched while she put her arm around
him. When it was done I helped Carmen hold him up while
he died."

"You bled him into the sink?"

"Does that make it worse?" Somehow the thought of an act so ruthless surprised me. Then I thought about the bullet ripping into Bull's gut and it didn't seem so ruthless anymore.

"No, of course not. Never mind. I'm not thinking very well. It takes me by surprise. Then you put the duffel bag around him and stored him in the Pontiac."

"Don't, please," Carlotta said. "Yes, of course. We wanted to put him in Bull's lap and let him deal with it. We knew he couldn't do much. We made the dirty work for him. He could never expose us without ruining himself." The wind rose and fell around us.

Finally Carlotta said, "What would you have done with the heroin?"

"I told Rossiter I would return it to him," I said.

"For a price?"

"Yes." Carlotta looked at me.

"How did you know where it was hidden?" Carlotta turned and stood with her back to me, looking out at the park. The white cotton ruffled in the breeze. Her back was very straight.

"Oh, that. Well, I had a few days to think after I got my brains caved in and a finger lopped off. I started thinking about you, about Saturday night, and about how quickly things were happening around me. Then I remembered you there on Saturday in the sunlight, kneeling in the roses, working the earth. Then it didn't make sense anymore after talking to you about roses. You were mulching and pretending to prune. You had a trowel and pruning knife. But you don't mulch and prune roses on the last day of August. Sure, maybe you do a watering, spray for hairy bugs. But you don't mulch. So, I decided you probably buried the heroin under the Texas Beautiful."

"I forgot about your grandfather and his rose pills."

"It doesn't matter," I said. It didn't.

"Why take the heroin this way?" she asked. Her voice was gentle, almost diaphanous.

"Because I killed the Bull tonight. Shot him. Right in the gut, too. Didn't give him a chance. So I wanted something for myself."

Carlotta said nothing. There were worlds moving behind her eyes. She took a long, deep breath. "He's dead?"

"If he's not, I'm in a world of shit. When he gets out of the hospital, he's gonna come after me and he's gonna be mad."

"No, please," Carlotta said in a trembling voice. "Please, not now."

"I'm sorry. You're right. I killed him tonight, Carlotta. He's dead and I'm glad as hell."

"Oh," she said. Then she held me and I could feel her shake. She gulped tears back. "No, I won't. I've wanted this for so long." After a while she said, "I have to go. What about the heroin?"

"I don't know," I said. "It doesn't matter much to me now. I expect the cops. I expect Rossiter. Whoever gets to me second is going to find bleached bones anyhow. Carlotta, I only made the deal with Rossiter because I thought I could make some money without hurting you. I didn't give a damn about anything else. It was Mitch Roberts I was thinking about. I figured if you could get what you wanted, so could I. So I shot the son of a bitch in his fat belly and came looking for the heroin. Now, go on."

She kissed me and it felt like the last one forever. "I have to go. I have to take care of Carmen. Maybe," she said, then stopped.

"Yeah, maybe. Get on." I smiled at her.

She got halfway down the porch steps. "What will happen?" she said.

"I don't know. I'm glad you're getting out. Go. Quick." Carlotta came back up the steps and kissed me. I was not going to tell her my problems with Rossiter. They were mine; I made them. Then she was gone into the darkness. I heard her open the shed doors and start the Thunderbird. I got out my last Lucky and watched the red taillights disappear down Nims and across the bridge. A feeling of enormous weariness settled over me then. Tired of greasy spoons, easy friendship, and the casual drunkenness that passed for sociability. Tired of the bruised summer days when you couldn't get your breath and the sterile winter when the clapboard and the dirt showed through. Tired of this helpless, brutal town lived in by helpless, brutal people with a knack of overlooking the obvious. I knew why I hadn't told Carlotta about Rossiter's threats. I didn't give a damn. Let him come. I would take him out if I could. It was a helpless, brutal idea.

I drove past the old Southwest Grease Factory and along the right field wall of the ballpark. I stopped for muscatel and cigarettes, then went home to a warm shower and a smoke.

I rocked on the porch. Across the street banks of lights glowed above the stadium and the sound of the organ bounced around the stands. People filed out of the gates with their hats and pennants and souvenir bats and drifted to their cars. It was the last game of the season and the public-address announcer thanked the fans and the players in that strong, confident echo that fills ballparks everywhere. Moths circled in the wavy currents of air and light, and there was one last, wistful cheer for little Joe Koppe who got player of the month. When the parking lot was empty and the ground crew had turned off all but one last bank of lights over the left-field wall, I sat in red-striped shorts and Marlon Brando T-shirt, rocking and pouring back tumblers of muscatel from a green gallon jug. I had the Browning tucked next to me beneath a spaghetti-stained tea towel. My feet balanced on the porch rail and pointed east. Between my toes I could see a sign that said Pepsi in red and blue. If a guy hit the Pepsi sign on the nose, he got a free dinner at Marvin Gardens on Harry Street. The sweet-and-sour at Marvin Gardens was like pancake dough sopped in lemonade, and to get that unlucky you had to hit a ball 378 feet on a dead line to left center. I think Covington did it once that season. I wondered if he ate the soggy chow mein.

I didn't think about Rossiter and his pals Hook Nose and Rushmore. I slid muscatel down and felt the warmth and freedom descend from my neck to my hands. I studied the plastic chess set, then got out a collection of games played by Steinitz in Germany during the 1890s. I was ten moves into a baroque queen's gambit when a dusty Plymouth braked hard and squealed around the corner onto Sycamore, finally coming to rest against the front curb. The headlights stayed lit and a rumpled man in a squashed linen suit staggered out the passenger door. In the dim light, I saw Andy's face, flushed and twisted. He stumbled when he got to the porch steps, then stopped and collected himself.

"Mitch," he said. "It's me." He took a couple of deep breaths.

"Come on up. I been expecting cops. You count as one of those. You here on business?"

Andy scaled the last two porch steps and held onto an edge of fusty white railing. "Sit?" he asked. When I said yes he collapsed into a slag heap with his back to a peeling post and his hands cupped between his legs. He looked beat and soused. "Business," he said. "Well, I don't know. I just don't goddamn know."

"What you need is some muscatel and a cigar. I got the muscatel, you got the cigars in your front pocket."

"Sure," he said. "That's what I need." I poured muscatel into a tumbler and put in some ice from a baking dish I had stashed full of cubes underneath the rocker. When I handed him the glass he took a big tug at it, then took five minutes to get his cheap Corona going with some soggy matches. He looked better when he had it under control.

"Business?" I asked again. There was a long silence while Andy looked at the darkened ballpark.

"You know," he said, "we didn't get to one doubleheader all goddamn season. That's a goddamn shame." He puffed the Corona. "I guess that's not the question." More Corona smoke.

He put his eyes on the floor between my knees. "I just came from over at the Bull's house. Some old lady puts in a call about two hours ago. She thinks she hears something. So a couple of boys run out that way. The old dame says she thinks she heard a shot but she can't be sure. Her old man says it's a backfire. Says she's crazy. Our boys look around and notice that Bull's Packard is nestled in its bunk, but there isn't any lights up in the palace. Well, it's pretty early for the Bull to be beddy-bye. They pound on his door. Nothing. Finally, they get out to the garage and what do you think they fucking find?" Andy lifted his eyes to mine and smiled a disconnected smile. His eyes floated like beach balls in the surf.

"Armadillos," I said. "Goddamn armadillos."

"Yeah, that's right. And you know what else?" I shook my head. "They found old Bull. Colonel Granger, head of fucking Vice. But he was one dead son of a bitch. He was so dead he'll never be the same again. And you know, Mitch, some bastard put a slug between his legs and let him bleed to death. Whole damn front seat full of blood. Buckets and buckets of it. Jesus!" Andy took a long drink of muscatel and we both sat quietly.

"So you had a few belts."

"Yeah," he said. "So I talked to the doctor. Then I had a few belts. He was a cop, you know. Like me." I put the chess set down beside the rocker. There was nothing to say.

"Doc said he hadn't been dead two or three hours. Had a big slug in his belly. What I hear, it's a 9mm. Must have hurt like hell for a while. It's like those guys I find down in the parking lots on Broadway with their guts spilled out like a busted watermelon. Uglier than shit." Andy had sobered. He pulled his tie off his shoulder and sucked at the stubby cigar he clenched in his teeth. There was look of sudden thoughtfulness on his face. He ran his stubby fingers through the shock of red hair sprouting on his head. "You own a Browning, don't you, Mitch?" he asked.

"Oh, that's fine. That's just fucking fine. You come around again. Sucking. You got something to say, for God's sake, say it. Say it." Andy drained his muscatel and held the tumbler out. I poured it full. I took a drink myself.

"I can't help the way it comes out, Mitch. I'm a cop. Okay."

Francis poked his triangle head around one of the porch posts. He meowed and jumped into my lap. "Yeah, I own a Browning," I said. "The Bull was a son of a bitch, Andy."

"He was a son of a bitch and he was a cop. Jesus, I got it bad, Mitch. I tell you something. I started looking over the body. Out of reflex, doing the stuff a cop does. There were things that didn't make sense." Andy put his back against a post and relit the Corona. He talked to the sky, letting smoke drift away from his freckled face.

Francis purred. I covered a finger with muscatel and let him lick it. He preferred Montrachet.

"I'm talking to the doctor," Andy said, "and he says come over and look at this. So, he shows me the Bull's ankle. Damn thing broke in half. And I say, so what? And the doc rolls up Bull's pants leg. Four, five, maybe six big bruises, a couple of deep lacerations. Cuts and bruises. The fucking guy is playing the *Tell* overture on this ankle. Cuts and bruises on top of a jagged break. Then I get to thinking. Some guy is bouncing that fucking door up and down on Bull's ankle and it was a Ping-Pong game. Mashed the son of a bitch, then torqued it and broke it. Now why would a guy do something like that?" Andy stopped.

"I don't know. You tell me, Andy," I said.

"Oh, yeah," Andy said, "Bull had money on him and a big watch. No robbery."

"Maybe the guy gets scared. Loses his head."

"Right, sure," Andy said. "He gets so scared he hangs around bouncing a door up and down on Bull's ankle. Scared as a fucking snake." I poured muscatel. Andy had his tumbler out. I filled it. "I'm looking at the doc and he's looking at me. So we are thinking the same thing. Some guy hides in the garage and catches the Bull from behind and pops him on the ear, but not enough to really hurt him. Just a tap. Bop. Then the Bull is down and has his ankle in the door, or maybe the guy puts it in there for him. Then he shoots the Bull, or maybe he plays a game and breaks an ankle while the Bull is alive. Probably that, says the doctor. By the bleeding and bruising he can tell, he says. So we got some psycho? Or we got a guy with a bad grudge, some guy out of stir with a crease in his balls? I don't know, the doc says. I think we got somebody very cool here who knew just what he was doing and why. That, he says, is just what we don't know. We got the how. Now, he says, go home and make a list of people who hate Colonel Bull Granger enough to kill him. He snickers. Take a couple of pencils, he says. And he laughs."

The left-field lights went out suddenly, leaving Andy and me silhouetted by the yellow light smeared on the dirty blinds behind us. Francis rolled onto his back and put his feet out. I scratched and he purred and I drank muscatel and Andy smoked his cigar and the old guy who chalks the baselines came out of the press gate and got in his pickup and drove slowly up Sycamore and into the neon haze of West Douglas.

We were well into the gallon. "So . . . you made the list?"

"Maybe," he said. "I took a pint of rye on a ride around town anyway. You see, Mitch, there's something bothering me that makes sense, but I don't want it to. So I drink some rye, but it still makes sense no matter how hard I try. You want to know?"

"Sure," I said. "Spill it."

"Gimme another one first." I filled his tumbler and put some fresh ice on top. He shook it and looked through the glass with one eye shut. "I tell you a story," he said finally. He slurred a little. Not much. "I'm a kid, see. Pretty new on the force. I got this shiny tail and a nice, shiny new badge and a shiny new wife and a shiny new house and I figure I'm gonna make the whole fucking world safe for fucking Joe Citizen."

Andy gulped muscatel. He was getting shaky. He didn't drink much rye or muscatel and it was hitting him like a sledge on the forehead. "So I get on Vice. Hell, that's pretty good duty, they told me. You don't sit around a desk all day, and there's some action and a chance to make stripes and get somebody's attention. That's when I get hooked up with Bull. He's a detective. Real hotshot. We're all supposed to kiss his ass, I guess, and learn how to be tough. After a while, it's not so hot. He pushes people. He does it for kicks. For fucking fun. He's got us licking his boots and after a couple of years it's no fun being a cop anymore because we just sneak around town taking bribes and pushing people in the goddamn face. But I do it, goddamn it. I got kids and a new house and I'm making stripes and I'm getting to be a rotten cop. Something happens and I'm no fucking good anymore. I'm standing outside that Packard and there's blood everywhere and I realize it's been ten goddamn years and I'm rotten as he was because everywhere he went, there I was to pick up his shitass garbage. It makes me sick."

"Take it easy, Andy," I said.

"You know something, Mitch? I don't talk to Elaine. Come and go and go and come and go. Jesus, she can't even look me in the eye. I don't goddamn blame her." Andy pulled a rag end of coat from under himself and leaned back against the post. "I tell you another story. Another one. This one is a real beaut."

"Okay."

"I'm still in uniform. It's late in the Forties sometime. I'm either driving for the Bull or doing his backup work. Me and this other guy. So one day we are out cruising when the Bull spots this colored chick pays him protection. Hooker. She works down Grove Street and she's been up and down more times than a yo-yo. You run her in and she bounces back. But she don't get in any brushes, not in any cons or heavy push-arounds. She just works her shit and lays the bread on her pimp and the Bull. But the Bull hassles her. This chick breaks a honky off in Bull's ear. It hit him wrong, and he runs her in. We get down to the station house and the Bull is in the lead car. Me and this other guy are driving the chick. We don't know what to tell her. So I get out and walk over to the station-house door and wait. Bull opens the door of the squad car and yanks this chick partway out. He gets her ankle in the fucking door. She's screaming. And I'm standing there and the Bull breaks her ankle. It makes me sick. And I just stand there. I don't do anything. Nothing. Bull drags her upstairs and beats the shit out of her and charges her with soliciting and resisting. Jesus! I didn't say anything. But, you know, that ain't really the story. All the time I'm standing there by the station-house door, I can see Bull's wife and stepdaughter on the sidewalk across the street going nuts. Carlotta and Bull's wife. I forget her name. Anyway, they are crying and carrying on, watching this whole scene. Now, you can probably understand that when I see Bull's ankle busted off in that car door, it leads me to think about Carlotta Granger. How she stood there watching the Bull pull this number on that colored chick and how her old lady took a dive out that sixth-floor window. You see how I would start thinking about that?"

"Andy, I can see how you would start thinking. You got any official-type thoughts?"

"For starters, I don't figure a woman the size of Carlotta Granger can hold that door shut and bounce on it hard enough to break the Bull's ankle. I don't figure she can handle a big 9mm automatic and shoot a man like that. I could be wrong, but I don't think so." Then he said, "Hell of a deal, we won the goddamn pennant. You know that?"

"Ten games," I said. I rocked back. "I killed the son of a

bitch. I got in the garage and broke his damn ankle and killed him."

"Jesus! You killed him for her? I mean you got in there and shot Bull because of Carlotta?"

"No," I said. "Not because of her. Because of this shit." I picked up my left hand and held out the bandage. Andy took hold of my forearm and ran his fat hand along my thumb.

"I wasn't paying any attention."

I leaned forward and bent my head down.

"He did that to you?" Andy said.

"Him or his buddies. You know about being pushed in the face, how there were all those nameless bastards pushed in the face? Hell, I was one of them. Only I pushed back."

"That's it? You pushed back."

"That's it. The fucking historical dialectic got the son of a bitch. Fucker ran head-on into the world historical spirit. And the world historical spirit was in a fucking bad mood." Andy laughed. "So what are you going to do, Andy?"

Andy shook his red head and stuck the wet cigar in his mouth. He picked up the pocket chess set and studied it. I handed him the book of Steinitz games.

"Yeah," he said. "Fucking Viennese Jew, right?" Steinitz was world champion for twenty years. Maybe the first you could really pick out who beat everybody in sight and didn't give a shit about anything except chess.

"Of course," Andy said, "I remember this game. It's the one where that son of a bitch moves his major pieces around for sixteen or eighteen moves and then gets them all back on the first row, except in different positions. His damn knights are on the wrong squares and the bishops are shitting their pants in the corners. His opponent didn't know what the hell to think. You remember what he said about all that?"

"Sure," I said. "'Why do you move that way?' the opponent asked. Steinitz glowered in unutterable contempt.

'You've seen a monkey observe a man wind a watch, I presume?'" Then Steinitz crushed his confused opponent, stalked from the club room in disgust, and wound up his old age in an insane asylum on Long Island, forgotten and abused. He bore bad, new ideas.

"Hell, I'm gonna go home," Andy said, "and kiss my wife. I'm gonna take a shower and see if I can't untangle all those goddamn pieces from the back row." He drained the muscatel from his tumbler and put it down on the railing. He scratched Francis on the back. "I feel like shit," he said. "I don't know what the hell to do with myself." He dropped the Corona in the catalpa beans and started down the stairs. "How did those guys get you anyway, you dumb shit?"

"Sunday evening," I said. "Out back of the office. I wasn't paying attention. Thought I had the world on a string, sitting on a rainbow. You know?"

"Sunday evening?" Andy said. He stepped back on the porch and stopped. He pushed a red wave from his eye. "Hey, Mitch. Jesus!" he said.

"Yeah?"

"Sunday evening. All evening. I was with those guys. Bull and Carl over at his place, playing poker like we do on the first Sunday of every month. This time they were talking about Frankie and one of their shipments and what the hell to do. They'd go in the other room and have these confabs, then come back and play some poker and drink. They didn't go anywhere. Gomez was driving a scrap truck to Texas. He left town Sunday afternoon."

I stopped thinking and let the pain and surprise settle. I felt drained and ugly. Carlotta. Jesus! On that Saturday afternoon we spent drinking, I told her about my life on the farm and about my mother and grandmother there. She knew I spent the early evening in the back of my office, sitting under the mimosa, smoking and relaxing. She knew about my run-in with Bull and about the threat I made to kill him if he touched me. When I phoned her Sunday evening she was out. She waited for me. Carlotta killed Frankie and she had killed the Bull and I was the puppet.

"You okay, Mitch?" Andy said.

"I'm just fine. I'm tired. I feel like the monkey who looks at a guy winding a watch."

"I know what you're thinking," he said. "It might not be."

"Yeah, it might not."

Andy started for his Plymouth. "We gotta get off the goddamn back row," he said. "You know, I got a feeling the cops are going to be stumped on this cop-killing deal." He got in the Plymouth and started the engine and drove slowly back to Maple and disappeared around the corner.

The night was finally still. I rocked and drank and smoked and played chess. At midnight Orion rose in the east above the gray outfield walls, above the line of box-cars on the Santa Fe tracks. I tensed when a white Cadillac stopped in front. There were two figures in the front seat and I could see the outline of Hook Nose on the passenger side. I pulled the Browning onto my lap and covered it with the dirty tea towel. I was drunk enough to believe that I could take Hook Nose out before he got up the steps.

Hook Nose had on the same pinstripe suit and white flower at the lapel. When he got to the steps he stopped and said, "You are a lucky punk." He threw two white envelopes my way. "Here," he said. "Count it."

I leaned down and picked up the envelopes. Inside was ten thousand in crisp hundred-dollar bills. Carlotta, I thought again.

Hook Nose turned. "The boss says this is your first and last adventure. You turn up again, anytime, anyplace, we put your fucking lights out, no questions." Hook Nose got back in the Cadillac. The car sped into the night.

I sat there all night, drinking muscatel. Just before dawn the Steffen's milkman strode briskly onto the porch with his rack of bottles and load of cottage cheese. He looked me over once and hurried away. Green gallon of muscatel, red-striped shorts, sweaty T-shirt, and Browning 9mm automatic pistol. The birds twittered for half an hour. The sun broke out. People went to work. Around ten, Mrs. Thompson poked her frazzled head around the corner of the porch. She saw me and hobbled up the steps. She wore the same dirty housecoat as always and her white hair stuck out in all directions. Her head bobbed nervously. Like a poor sparrow.

"Mr. Mitch! Mr. Mitch!" she screamed. Her eyes were halos of uncertainty. "Oh, Mr. Mitch!"

She handed me a pad and pencil. "What day is it?" she yelled.

I wrote: THURSDAY. DON'T WORRY. I'LL TAKE CARE OF YOU. SIT WITH ME?

Mrs. Thompson took the note, read it, and smiled. From a fold of her housecoat she took a big red apple and held it out to me with her withered, wrinkled hand. I took the apple, stood up, and pulled another rocker up next to mine. I got Mrs. Thompson to sit down and we rocked and I smoked and she looked serenely happy.

While we rocked the day became hot and dead still. I thought about a little piece of land for sale up by Thompson Falls, Montana, where a guy could fish for trout even with nine fingers. Then I thought about the bamboo fly rod I could finally afford. Last of all I thought about my ex-wife, Linda. When it was that hot and dead still, I always did.

# JONATHAN VALIN

## NATURAL CAUSES       68247-8/$2.95
When ace detective Harry Stoner is hired to find out who killed a TV soap writer, he uncovers a slick world of high finance and low morals, the perfect setting for greed, jealousy, and murder.
"A superior writer...Smart and sophisticated."
*The New York Times Book Review*

## DAY OF WRATH       63917-3/$3.50 US/$4.50 Can
Harry Stoner takes on the simple case of a teenage runaway—and finds himself on a bloody trail leading from the sleazy barrooms of Cincinnati to the luxurious penthouse of a well-known socialite.
"An out-and-out shocker." *Chicago Sun-Times*

## DEAD LETTER       61366-2/$3.50 US/$4.50 Can
The Cincinnati private eye is pitted against the rivalries and plots of a hateful family, who soon have him involved in a gruesome murder case.
"A classic puzzle of motives." *Newsweek*

## FINAL NOTICE       57893-X/$3.50 US/$4.50 Can
Private eye Harry Stoner must find a psychotic killer who mutilates art photos of beautiful women before moving on to living victims.
"One of the scariest, most pulse-pounding thrillers you'll ever read...A superior mystery." *Booklist*

## LIME PIT       55442-9/$3.50 US/$4.50 Can
Harry Stoner tries to right the wrongs of a heartless city as he searches for a 16-year-old runaway who has disappeared into Cincinnati's seamy netherworld of prostitution and porn.
"THE LIME PIT is done right!" *New York Daily News*

---